OUR
ISLAND STORY

Vincent McDonnell from County Mayo lives near Newmarket, County Cork. In 1989 he won the GPA First Fiction Award, after being recommended by Graham Greene. He has published four other non-fiction titles and seven novels for children. Winner of numerous prizes, and shortlisted for the RAI Awards, he has been writer in residence at many venues and gives workshops and readings throughout Ireland.

For my sister Tina, Tommie and family and for my sister Theresa, Gerry and family

OUR
ISLAND STORY

Vincent McDonnell

The Collins Press

FIRST PUBLISHED IN 2011 BY
The Collins Press
West Link Park
Doughcloyne
Wilton
Cork

A Cataloguing in Publication data record is available for this title
from the British Library.

ISBN: 978-184889-118-0

Typesetting by The Collins Press

Typeset in Garamond 12 pt and Candara 16 pt

Printed in Malta by Gutenberg

Contents

1
Back to the Beginning

When you think of Ireland, do you imagine a country of lofty mountains and rolling hills, of babbling rivers and green glens? It's how many people think of Ireland: a country of mists and myths and legends, where fairies live in fairy forts and at night dance around a solitary thorn tree to the plaintive music of a fiddle, where leprechauns, small men dressed in green, make beautiful leather shoes with silver buckles and guard their pots of gold. Ireland is also the country of the banshee, whose cries can be heard at night when someone dies.

It is a country of poets and singers and musicians. We have storytellers too, whose stories recount the brave deeds of heroes of old like Fionn MacCumhaill and Oisín and the Fianna; and of Queen Maeve of Connacht who fought a great battle over the ownership of the Brown Bull of Cooley. The stories also tell the tragedy of the Children of Lir, who were turned into swans, and the exploits of Setanta, who slew the hound of Culainn and became known afterwards as Cú Chulainn, or Culainn's Hound. The stories also tell of ghosts and goblins and giants, and of dark-faced men called pookas who roam the countryside on moonless nights.

But there is another Ireland, a country that has survived invaders and marauders, and which has been conquered and ruled by a foreign power. Great battles have been fought on its soil and tens of thousands of its people have died in those conflicts. Terrible famines have ravaged the country. In one such famine, known as The Great Hunger, millions died of starvation and disease, or fled the country in terror. So many Irish men and woman emigrated to every part of the globe seeking a new life for themselves and their families that today Ireland is known throughout the whole world.

We have our own language and our native games of football and hurling, the latter having been played for thousands of years. Over two millenia ago, great sporting gatherings called the Tailteann Games were held. They included athletics and wrestling, as well as storytelling and drama. It is claimed that the modern Olympic Games, which first took place in Greece more than 2,000 years ago, were based on Ireland's Tailteann Games.

Five thousand years ago, the largest settled farming community yet discovered in the world existed at the Céide Fields at Ballycastle in County Mayo. At that time, too, the people who then lived in County Meath built Newgrange, one of the first and largest man-made structures ever built on earth. It existed even before the pyramids were built in Egypt. The people who built Newgrange had no machinery. All they had were their hands and stone tools. Yet they were an intelligent people and knew how to measure the movement of the earth and the sun precisely.

The people who lived at the Céide Fields, or who built Newgrange, did not know how to write. They have left no written evidence of their existence – only their buildings and tools, and evidence of where they once lived. But thousands of years later, when the people who then lived in Ireland did know how to read and write, they wrote some of the most beautiful handwritten books in the whole world.

From AD 400 to AD 1200, a time in Europe now referred to as the Dark Ages, is known in Ireland as the age of saints and scholars, or The Golden Age. During the first 400 years of The Golden Age, Irish monks, using homemade inks and quills, wrote the largest number of illuminated, or illustrated, manuscripts that exists anywhere in the world from that time. The most magnificent of all those illuminated manuscripts is the Book of Kells, which can be seen in Trinity College, Dublin.

At this time Irish goldsmiths and silversmiths were also creating beautiful items of gold and silver, inlaid with jewels, and decorated with enamel. In 1868, a boy digging potatoes in Ardagh, County Limerick, found one of those items, a chalice, buried beneath a thorn bush. It is now known as the Ardagh Chalice, and regarded as a true wonder of the world. It can be seen at the National Museum of Ireland. Two other equally magnificent items have also been found. They are the Derrynaflan Chalice and the Tara Brooch.

During this period, the people of Britain and Europe were living in a Dark Age. It began with the fall of the Roman Empire, which was destroyed by tribes called Visigoths and Vandals. This event led to wars in Europe, as different tribes fought for supremacy. While wars raged, there was little time for learning. Ireland, which had not been part of the Roman Empire, avoided these wars, and here learning flourished and Irish missionaries brought this learning to the peoples of Britain and Europe. It is also claimed that Saint Brendan, one of those missionaries, sailed in a leather boat to what we now call America 1,000 years before Christopher Columbus.

Yet in world terms, Ireland is a very young country, probably still a teenager. The first people arrived here only about 9,000 years ago. By then people had spread out from Africa to Europe and Britain. They had crossed the Bering Straits into North America and made their way down that continent to South America. By this time too they had arrived in Australia. So why hadn't they come to Ireland, I hear you ask? To answer that question we must go back more than 9,000 years, back to a time which we will describe as the beginning of history in Ireland.

History, I hear you complain with a great sigh of resignation. History can be boring. It's all about dates and battles and the names of kings and queens who are long dead. Well, yes, I agree, history is about those things. But it's also about much more than that. It's about the men and women and children from the past and how they lived and died. Those children didn't have to go to school but that doesn't mean that their life was easy. I'm sure they had to work hard doing chores just as you do today. In fact, they were just like you, with the same hopes and dreams as you have today – to be happy and contented and to live a long and interesting life.

Today, you usually learn about history from books. Ever since man discovered a means of writing he has left records. The first writings were scratched on tablets of clay. Men also inscribed the exploits of their peoples and their rulers on buildings and on tombs and on stone. Later, men discovered ways of making paper. The Egyptians made paper from papyrus reeds and used a pictorial type of writing called hieroglyphics. They also inscribed hieroglyphics on their tombs and buildings. From all those writings we can learn about the people who lived at that time.

The first people who came to Ireland did not have writing, so how can we know their history? Or how can we know what Ireland was like before those first people arrived? Luckily, there are ways, other than writing, of discovering what a country was like thousands of years ago, and how its people lived.

So let's go back to that time before people arrived in Ireland. It is a time when the country resembled Antarctica as we know it today, and almost the whole country was covered in a giant ice cap. Let's go back to what we call the Great Ice Age, just before the beginning of the exciting history of Ireland and its people.

2
Ireland's History Begins

Until 9,000 years ago there were no humans living in Ireland. People could not have survived because the climate was bitterly cold. It was so cold that most of the country was covered by a gigantic ice cap. This was hundreds of metres deep in places, especially in the northern part of the country. It was so heavy that it pressed down the land, just like what happens to a piece of foam rubber if you place a heavy book on it. We don't know why the country was so cold, but we know this icecap existed because it has left evidence behind of its presence.

Wherever there are icecaps, there are also glaciers. A glacier is a gigantic river of ice. As you know, rivers flow and so do glaciers, but they do not flow as fast as a river. A glacier moves so slowly that its movement is hardly noticeable. As it creeps forward, it gouges out the earth beneath and to each side of it, creating valleys and fjords in the process. Killary Harbour, a fjord on the border of Counties Mayo and Galway, was carved out by a gigantic glacier, and is the only fjord in Ireland.

As a glacier creeps forward, it collects debris – soil and ground-up rock and sand and grit. When it eventually melts it deposits this debris, which forms small round hills or long ridges. In Ireland these hills are called drumlins and the ridges are called eskers. Most of them are in the north of the country and many Irish place names have the word 'drumlin' or 'esker' in them. There is other evidence, too, for the presence of glaciers in Ireland. When they move across solid rock they scrape it, and we can still see these scrape marks today in various parts of the country.

So until around 10,000 years ago, Ireland was like Antarctica is today, though we did not have penguins in Ireland. In fact, during the

Great Ice Age, which is what we call that time, few animals could have survived the bitter cold.

Then the climate changed and the ice slowly melted. We don't really know why this happened, only that it did. With all that weight gone, the land must have given a great sigh of relief as it rose up, just like that piece of foam rubber when the book is lifted from it. At Courtmacsherry, County Cork, you can see beaches high above the beach on which you sunbathe or build sandcastles. This tells us that at the time of the Ice Age the land had been pressed down to the level of the raised beach. Ireland is still rising out of the sea, but so slowly that it will be thousands of years before there is a noticeable change.

Once the ice melted, vegetation grew. Gradually, over the next 1,000 years or so Ireland was covered with a giant forest. During this time one of the most amazing Irish animals lived – the giant elk or deer. He was 3 metres or more in height and his antlers were even wider. As the forest expanded, the elk became extinct. It is thought that his antlers were so wide that they caught in the branches of trees and he could no longer find food.

Other animals survived, like brown bears and wolves and foxes and wild boar. There were fish in the rivers and in the seas and, of course, there were birds. As the vegetation expanded there were fruits and nuts and tubers and fungi. There was an abundance of food for anyone who cared to come and hunt or fish, or gather fruit and nuts and fungi.

By this time, people lived throughout much of Europe and had found their way to Britain and other parts of the world. But, as yet, they had not travelled to Ireland. All that was about to change and the history of Ireland really begin.

We don't exactly know when the first humans came to Ireland, or where they came from. Some historians believe that the first people came from Greece and died of plague. Others believe that the first people were the Formorians, who were said to have come from Africa, and were descended from Noah. After them came the Fir Bolgs and still later the Tuatha Dé Danann, who were said to have magical powers. Then the Milesians came and conquered the Tuatha Dé Danann, who then retreated underground and became the fairies of Irish legends.

As this is clearly part of myth and legend, you can see that it's not easy to know the early history of the people who first came here. The stories about them were not written until thousands of years after they first came. Instead, the stories were passed down by word of mouth, and no doubt were added to and exaggerated so that it's difficult now to tell truth from myth.

But luckily there is physical evidence of the presence of the first people who came to Ireland long ago. This evidence exists at the places where they lived and died. In Ireland, these places are around the coast of County Antrim and further west at Mount Sandal in County Derry.

The nearest land to the County Antrim coast is the west coast of Scotland. So we assume that those first settlers came from there. On a clear day you can see the Irish coastline from Scotland. So the people who lived on the Scottish shores 9,000 years ago must have looked west many times and wondered about the land they could see across the sea.

These people were hunter-gatherers. They lived in tents made of animal skins or huts made of brush. They hunted and fished for their food and gathered berries, fruits and nuts, and fungi and edible roots. When animals and other food sources became scarce, they gathered up their belongings and moved on to where there was food. Because of this, they were used to moving to and exploring new places.

Now, all creatures are curious. Not only do they like to explore their own environment but they also like to explore the world about them. Just observe the behaviour of a new puppy. It will dash about the house, looking and sniffing at everything. If you open a cupboard, it will scamper inside to see what's in there. If you open a door it will rush through to see what lies beyond.

Humans are just as curious as any puppy. But they go further than mere curiosity. They ask questions. One day a man must have stood at the edge of the sea in Scotland, looked west to Ireland and wondered about that land. What sort of land was it? Who, if anyone, lived there? Should he travel there and explore it?

Can you picture him? He's probably not tall, because we think that people were smaller long ago. He's probably short and stocky, but strong and healthy too. There were few medicines in those times and if he became ill, or was injured, it was likely that he would die.

He's wearing simple breeches made of cured animal skins and probably some sort of vest or tunic, also made of skins. His feet are bare, or he may be wearing simple leather sandals, or leather thongs wrapped around his feet. His body is smeared with the juice of berries or with chalk, and almost certainly so is his face. He may have crude tattoos on his skin and even have body piercings, just as some people do today.

His hair is wild and matted and he's carrying a flint axe or spear and possibly a flint knife. For danger lurks all about. He might be attacked at any time by a wild animal or by men from another tribe living in the vicinity. Perhaps he and his tribe are in danger from other tribes who live close by, and he is thinking that he might find safety in that land across the sea.

At one time Ireland was joined to Scotland and you could walk from one country to another. We think that this was how all those animals came to Ireland when the ice began to melt. But by 9,000 years ago, that linking piece of land had become submerged beneath the sea as the ice melted and sea levels rose. This is why we assume that the first men who travelled to Ireland did so in a boat.

This may have been a dugout canoe, which is formed by gouging out the inside of a huge log and shaping one end into a V shape so that it will cut easily through the water. Or perhaps the boat had a simple wooden frame covered with animal skins and probably caulked (sealed) with pitch. Whichever it was, it would have been a very frail craft for a sea journey and those first humans who crossed the sea to Ireland must have been very brave indeed. Not only were they going to be at the mercy of the sea, but they didn't know whether they might encounter hostile people or fierce wild animals in the new land.

They would have planned for the journey, taking with them on the boat meat and fish and maybe nuts and edible roots. Water would have been essential, and they would have brought a number of boars' bladders filled with water, the openings carefully tied off so that none of the precious liquid should spill.

They would also have brought other essential items with them. These would have been cutters and scrapers made from flint. They would also have brought some flint-tipped spears and flint axes with which to defend themselves and for hunting when they reached land. It's possible that they also had some form of net, probably made from lengths of plaited strips of bark or even from animal sinews, with which they could catch fish. They would also have small pieces of flint and tinder with them so that they could light a fire when they arrived in the new land.

With other members of their group watching apprehensively from the edge of the water they would have launched their boat, scrambled aboard and with simple oars pulled away from the shore. They would have left at dawn on a calm summer morning with the intention of reaching their destination by nightfall. Perhaps the women and children were crying, unsure if they would ever see their loved ones again.

Though they did not write things down, nor paint pictures on the walls of caves, nor carve sculptures in stone, these people still left evidence of their existence. We have found their flint tools and the bones of the animals and fish they ate and the shells of the hazelnuts they gathered and the ashes from their cooking fires.

Just close your eyes for a moment and imagine them gathered around a huge blazing fire eating roast boar. You can almost smell it! When they've eaten, someone starts to recount the story of that day's hunt; or perhaps a hunt from the past. There's no sound to be heard except the crackle of the fire and the voice of the hunter as he recounts the moment when the boar charged and he thought he would be killed. As his voice drops at the moment of greatest suspense, everyone is listening enthralled. Just look at the faces of those children with their eyes wide open in amazement. Aren't they just like you as you watch an episode of your favourite programme on TV?

Now glance at a man or a woman sitting around that fire. Could they be your ancestors, or even mine? How can we know? Perhaps that storyteller is your great-great-great – imagine a page of greats – grandfather from 9,000 years ago. But he, too, had a father and a grandfather and a great-grandfather – and so we go on back further and further in time. How far back? Again we do not know.

Now do you see why those people from 9,000 years ago and those who came before them and after them are relevant to us today? It's why history is so important. History tells us about who we are and where we came from – it tells us about those people who lived and died thousands of years before we were even born. Without them, you see, we wouldn't exist.

Their history is our history, all 9,000 years of it. It's the link between all those people who have lived and us. In a thousand years from now people will look back at us and see us as part of history. And just as you wouldn't like them to think that we were of little importance, so we should not think that those who came before us are not important either.

So though history is all about the past, it is very relevant to us living here in the present too. And now that you realise this, sit back and let's see what happened to all those people who lived and died in Ireland over the past 9,000 years. At times it is a sad story, but it is also a thrilling and exciting story – the story of Ireland and its people.

3
The Age of Stone

The first people who came to Ireland lived during the Stone Age. We call it the Stone Age because the tools they used were made from stone. The Stone Age is divided into three periods – Old Stone Age, Middle Stone Age and New Stone Age – by the type of stone tools used. In the Old Stone Age simple tools were made from stone. By the Middle Stone Age tools were made from flint. During the New Stone Age, these flint tools were highly crafted. We know from tools found at the sites where those people first settled that they lived in the Middle Stone Age.

Over time, other people came to Ireland. They came from Scotland and other parts of Britain, and from Europe and Scandinavia. Gradually these people moved inland, hunting and gathering food. It is likely that those different groups met and fought each other, but it's equally likely that they became friends and joined together.

As their numbers increased it became more difficult to find sufficient food to feed everyone just by hunting and gathering. At some point these people began to settle in one place. They built houses of wood and stone and began to cultivate the land and grow crops. They also built elaborate tombs in which to bury their dead, and these can still be seen today in many parts of Ireland.

When we look at a map of the world, Ireland looks terribly small and insignificant. We might think that it played little part in the history of the world. But we would be wrong. Ireland has played a significant part in world history. Again we know this from the evidence the people left behind.

In the 1930s a teacher, Patrick Caulfield, was cutting turf near Ballycastle, County Mayo. As he dug deep in the bog he uncovered lines of stones. Now you or I might not think this odd and ignore it. But Patrick Caulfield realised that someone must have placed those stones in regular lines. As they were deep beneath the bog and it takes thousands of years for a bog to grow, he realised that whoever had placed these stones in straight lines must have done so a very long time ago indeed.

Later, his son Seamus Caulfield investigated further. He was a very clever man and he devised a means of checking out all the lines of stones so he didn't have to dig up thousands of acres of bog. Do you know what he did?

He got a long iron rod and marked if off in feet and inches. Then he walked through the bog pushing this rod into the soft peat. Whenever he struck stone he measured the depth on the rod and then placed a marker at the spot. Slowly he mapped out the lines of stones.

He realised that they were the remains of stone fences dividing off fields. Other stone formations he found were the remains of houses and other buildings. What lay beneath the bog was the remains of an ancient farming community. But how old was it? When had these people lived?

Scientists have many ways of dating old objects and measuring time. One method is carbon dating, which needs special instruments. A much more simple way is to count the rings in the cross-section of a tree. Each ring represents one year's growth. Using many different methods, scientists were able to date the age of this settlement. They discovered that it was over 5,000 years old, one of the oldest and largest settled farming communities ever found anywhere in the world. Now do you see how important a part Ireland has played in the history of the world? And it's not the only part. There is much, much more.

Were those people who lived in Ballycastle direct descendants of those who crossed over from Scotland? Are you and I descended from them? Right now, we don't really know. Perhaps they were new settlers who came from Britain, or maybe from Europe, and perhaps we are descended from them.

One day we may really know. Scientists have developed a way of identifying our genes, which are a kind of chemical we have in our bodies. We get these genes from our parents who got them from their parents

The Age of Stone

and so on. If scientists compared our genes with those of someone from thousands of years ago, they could tell if we were related. This science is called the science of DNA, and some day scientists will be able to trace our ancestors using DNA.

Then we will know whether our ancestors were those people who came from Scotland 9,000 years ago; or whether they were those people who built all those stone walls at Ballycastle; or whether we're related to people who settled at Lough Gur, County Limerick about 5,000 years ago. Or perhaps our ancestors lived in County Meath and built one of the oldest and most amazing structures in the whole world – the great tomb at Newgrange.

4
The Great Irish Tombs

One of the things the first people who lived on the earth must have wondered about is what happens to us when we die. Even though they were primitive people, they realised that human beings possessed a spirit or soul. They believed that this spirit or soul continued to exist after a person died, and so they had a great respect and reverence for their dead. Because of this, they built gigantic tombs in which to place the bones or ashes of their loved ones.

One of the most magnificent tombs in Ireland, or anywhere in the world, is the great tomb at Newgrange. It's called a passage-tomb because a passage, like a hallway, leads to a central chamber or room. The passage is built of gigantic standing stones, and is around 20 metres in length. It leads to the central chamber, which is also built of stone and has a massive stone roof. Even though it was built over 5,000 years ago, the roof is still intact and the chamber remains dry, which is a credit to the skills of those Stone Age builders. The complete structure is estimated to contain over 200,000 tonnes of stone. Can you imagine how much time, effort and hard work it must have taken to build?

The passage and central chamber were built first and were then covered over with stones and earth to create a flat-topped hill or mound. This mound is 11 metres high and has a diameter of 85 metres. Many of the stones used in the building have carvings on them, mostly spirals, and stones in the central chamber have carvings too. We do not know what these carvings mean; maybe they represent the sun, the moon or perhaps the stars. We do know that many ancient people worshipped the sun.

There is one more amazing testament to the skill and knowledge of the people who built the tomb. Above the entrance to the passage, there is a rectangular opening. When the tomb was discovered and excavated, this opening puzzled archaeologists. They could not figure out why it was there, or what purpose it served.

Now we know what purpose it serves. If you visit the tomb on the morning of 21 December – the winter solstice and the shortest day of the year – the sun's rays shine through the rectangular opening, all the way down the long passage, to illuminate the central chamber. It is the only day in the year in which this event occurs.

The people who built Newgrange had no clocks or sophisticated scientific instruments like those we have today. Yet they were able to calculate, by observing the movement of the earth relative to the sun, when the winter solstice was. When they built their magnificent tomb they were able to calculate exactly where to place the central chamber, and how to line up the passage and that rectangular box so that the sun's rays would light up the central chamber on the shortest day of the year. So these people were not only hard working, but extremely clever and intelligent.

We cannot be sure why they built the tomb so that the sun's rays light up the inner chamber. Was it to symbolise that the spirits of their loved ones buried in the chamber still lived? Or did they wish to mark the moment when the days would begin to grow longer and brighter and they could soon plant their crops again? Whatever the reason, the construction of Newgrange is an extraordinary feat of knowledge, engineering and cooperation.

But it is not the only tomb in Ireland. There are over a thousand tombs in the country dating from those earliest times, most of them of four different designs. One is the passage-tomb like that at Newgrange. Another is the wedge tomb, and there are many of those in the south and west of Ireland. These tombs, also built of stone, are wider and taller at the front and narrower and lower at the rear. They resemble a wedge which is why they have that name.

Another type of tomb is the portal tomb or dolmen, which resembles a leaning, three-legged stool. It consists of two giant standing stones at the front and a smaller standing stone at the back. On top of these three stones is placed a gigantic flat stone, called a capstone. The capstone of one dolmen in County Wicklow weighs over 10,000 kilograms. Again, can you imagine how much effort it must have taken to lift that stone into place? We don't know how it was done, but probably a ramp of stone and earth was built and the capstone was pulled up this ramp and over the three standing stones. Then the ramp was taken away. It must have taken many people and much time to do this, so we know that there were large groups of people living close to these tombs when they were built, and that they were willing to cooperate in building them.

The final type of tomb is the court tomb; most of these are in the northern part of Ireland. These tombs have huge stones forming a semi-circle at the entrance, which leads into a number of burial chambers.

Ashes and bones have been found in these tombs as well as objects like knives, axe heads and arrowheads, and objects carved from bone. They were probably placed there so that the spirits of those who had died could use them in the other world if they so wished. This was a common practice with the people who lived thousands of years ago, not only in Ireland, but elsewhere. In Egypt, the pharaohs were buried in gigantic tombs carved out of rock along with magnificent objects made of gold and precious stones. In fact the pyramids were built as tombs for pharaohs, just as Newgrange was built as a tomb for the important rulers of the people who built it. We know from those structures that the people revered their rulers and their dead, just as we still do today.

This is how we know how people lived in Ireland before anything was written down. We know they lived in communities in various parts of the island. The country was covered in forest so it would not have been possible to travel easily from one place to another. Rivers would have been one way of travelling; another would have been to sail around

The Great Irish Tombs

the coast. It is likely that there was little communication between the people living in different parts of the country. It is possible that those living along the coast had more contact with people living in Britain and Europe because they could travel across the sea by boat. We know there was trade between Ireland and Britain and between Ireland and Europe. Tools made from Irish flint have been found in Britain, while amber and pottery, which came from Europe, have been found in Ireland.

For the first 5,000 years, the people who lived in Ireland lived in the Stone Age. Then a great change came about. Man discovered metal. The Stone Age ended and the Bronze Age began.

5
The Bronze Age

The discovery of metal was a momentous event, not only in the history of Ireland, but also in the history of the world. As with many discoveries, we don't really know how this happened. Perhaps stone containing copper was placed in a fire. The copper then melted and flowed out and hardened when it cooled. Some clever person must have realised that the material could be made into a tool.

The first metal tools were made of copper. And though copper is a soft metal and quite weak, nevertheless it has great advantages over stone. The melted copper could be poured into clay moulds made in the shape of knives, chisels, axe-heads, arrowheads, spearheads and tools. Once the copper hardened, the tool could be removed from the mould. Copper tools could also be resharpened, which was a huge advantage over stone or flint.

Then another discovery was made, which would really improve the quality of the metal. If you mix a small amount of tin with copper you create a new material, called bronze. This is a much harder and more durable metal than copper, and is of such importance that it gives its name to a period in history: the Bronze Age. It began about 4,000 years ago and ended about 2,500 years ago.

We don't know if the people who lived in Ireland at that time discovered the secret of metal themselves, or whether that knowledge was brought to Ireland by others who came here. We do know that people, known as the Beaker People, came from Europe to Ireland at this time. They derive their name from a type of flat-bottomed beaker – a sort of cup – they made. Pottery, as you know, is made from fired clay and, like stone, does not rot. Some of this Beaker pottery, which has been found in Europe, has also been found in Ireland. So perhaps the Beaker People brought the secret of metal here.

During the Bronze Age, the climate in Ireland changed, and it became cold and wet. In these conditions, bog began to grow. We think that this is what happened at the Céide Fields and that it forced the people there to move away from the area. But bronze tools brought a huge advantage. With bronze axes, trees could be more easily cut down, providing more land on which to grow barley, oats and emmer, a type of wheat. This increase in the growing and harvesting of crops meant that communities became better off. But it brought its own problems. Communities now needed to defend themselves from enemies who might wish to take from them what they owned.

Communities used different means of defending themselves. They erected palisades – fences of hewn logs – around their villages, which were usually situated beside water. A regular supply of water was essential, so these villages were built near rivers or lakes. Sometimes, people built their house on an island in a lake and had a bridge linking the island to the surrounding land. The bridge could be taken up at night, or during an attack, thus preventing the attackers from reaching the house. If there was no island on the lake, the people constructed one with stones and rubble. These lake dwellings are called crannógs and one of the best-known crannógs in Ireland is at Lough Gur, County Limerick.

There is one other reason why people built near water – water is needed for cooking. Now you might think that they used metal pots filled with water in which to boil their meat. But they did not. Instead, they dug a square pit beside the water source, lined it with oak planks and filled it with water. They then lit a huge fire in which they heated stones. When the stones were hot, they were dropped into the pit and this caused the water to boil. When the water was boiling, meat wrapped in straw was hung from a wooden beam placed across the pit. Hot stones were added to keep the water boiling until the meat was cooked.

This type of cooking pit is called a fulacht fiadh and there are thousands of them dotted around Ireland. I once saw a reconstruction of one and it only took about thirty minutes to bring the huge pit of water to the boil. The piece of mutton took the same amount of time to cook as it would in your kitchen at home. I tasted the meat when it was cooked and it was delicious!

As these Irish communities got bigger, they began to build hill forts or raths. These were built on a hilltop which meant that you had a good view over the countryside below and could see an enemy approaching. These forts or raths, which were circular in shape, were protected by banks of piled-up earth. Another type of fort was the cashel, or caher; here, walls built of stone were used for protection. It is estimated that there are the remains of over 40,000 forts or cashels in Ireland, and many place names have fort, rath, caher, or cashel in them. Perhaps there is one near to where you live.

A family, or group of related families, would live in the fort, protected from attack by the earthen banks or stone walls. One fort in County Wicklow had four banks, or walls, for protection. This tells us that the people who lived there needed a lot of protection. This may have been from other people who lived in Ireland, or from raiders from Britain or from Europe.

From the beginning of time men have wanted what other men possess. One of the things that they most covet is gold, and when they become crazy with their desire for gold, we say that they are suffering from gold fever. Gold has always held a special fascination for men, and still does to this very day. When an athlete wins at the Olympics he or she is presented with a gold medal. When a couple get married, they exchange gold rings. Though we have even more precious metals than gold today, it is still regarded as the most valuable and desired metal on earth. It gleams and dazzles when light shines on it, is hard wearing, does not rust or tarnish, and lasts a long time. These are the reasons why it is so valued today, and why it was so valued thousands of years ago.

Such a valuable metal was not used by our ancestors to make weapons or tools. Instead, they made ornaments like gold collars, necklaces and arm and leg bracelets called torcs and another type of necklace called a lunula. They also made earrings, and pins for women to wear in their hair, fasteners for their clothing and discs that resembled blazing suns.

The Bronze Age

Thousands of years ago, there was much gold in Ireland and one of the largest gold mines in the country was in County Wicklow.

When raiders attacked Irish settlements, they were not only seeking weapons and slaves and food and goods, but also gold. It is probable that due to these raiders, the forts and raths and cashels were built. It is likely that the well-defended fort in County Wicklow was built because the people who lived there had large amounts of gold and objects made of gold because of the goldmine in that county.

These raiders did not remain in the country. Instead, they took whatever they wanted and returned to their homes. But other people did come to stay in the 6,000 years following the arrival of those first settlers from Scotland. We know that the Beaker People came, as did the people who lived at Lough Gur. But none of those was to have the effect on the country, and on those already living here, than the Celts, who first came here about 2,500 years ago. It was a turbulent period, not only in Irish history, but in world history. Man had discovered iron, which is a much better metal than bronze, and those who possessed iron weapons conquered those who still used bronze. With the discovery of iron, the Bronze Age came to an end and we entered what is called the Iron Age.

6
The Celts

The Celts came from Europe and were once part of a great Celtic Empire. They spoke a language from which our Gaelic language has come. They were a tall, proud people with light reddish hair. They were warriors, and their powerful physique and iron weapons gave them superiority over other smaller and less well-armed people. Despite this, they were driven out of Europe by other more powerful tribes.

It is likely that the Celts introduced the art of horsemanship to Ireland. Very elaborate horses' bits made of bronze, and dating from around 2,000 years ago, have been found here. Wide tracks made of hewn wooden planks have also been found. These must have been built to allow easy passage of wheeled vehicles, probably horses pulling carts.

Some historians claim that the Celts had chariots similar to those of the Romans. Blades, which may have been fixed to the wheels of a chariot, have been found in Ireland. So it is possible that the Celts did have chariots. They would have been familiar with Roman chariots and may have copied them. If they used horses and chariots in their warfare, they would have had a huge advantage over the native population who were, for the most part, farmers.

Historians once thought that a large army of Celtic warriors invaded Ireland about 2,500 years ago and conquered the country. Now they no longer believe this. They think that the Celts came in smaller groups over a period of hundreds of years and gradually subdued the people already living here. As often happens in these situations, the Celts and the natives intermarried. Eventually they all merged together and became the ancestors of the Irish people we are today. The Celts named the country *Ériu*, or as it is known today, Erin, and Ireland is now the only remaining independent Celtic nation in the world.

As well as iron tools and weapons, the Celts brought to Ireland a certain style in decoration called the La Tène style. It is named after a place in Switzerland where a great many objects in that style were found. The Celts were master-craftsmen in metal and leather, and especially in gold. They wore gold neck decorations, and also rings and bracelets, some of which were worn around the ankle. They painted and engraved designs on the objects they made, but we do not understand what these designs mean. They were also masters at carving, and carved their designs on stone. One of the best examples of their stone carving is the Turoe Stone, near Loughrea, County Galway.

The Celts were a religious people and had many gods. They believed that these gods dwelt on mountains, and in rivers and trees and woods. Their best-known god was named Lug. The festival of Lughnasa was held in his honour on the first day of August every year. Today, the Irish name for August is still Lughnasa, and is a link back to our ancient ancestors.

The Celts were what we call pagans, and they had priests who were known as druids. A stone carving of druids found in France shows two tall men in long robes, and with long hair and beards. One is wearing a headdress of flowers and leaves and is carrying a ceremonial mace. The druids were revered and no doubt feared, for ordinary people believed they had magical powers. People in those ancient times probably danced and chanted around fires to the beat of drums, and played simple music on whistles made of hollow bones. They also had bronze horns, which were so elaborate that they were almost certainly played only on important religious or ceremonial occasions. The largest collection of Celtic horns in the world has been found in Ireland. When they were first found no one knew how to play them. But recently, people have learned how to play them.

These religious celebrations were held at special times of the year. The most important of these times were the spring and autumn equinoxes and the summer and winter solstices. These dates mark specific points in the earth's orbit around the sun, and are closely associated with the seasons. The equinoxes mark the two times when there are equal hours of daylight and darkness. The summer solstice marks the time when the days begin to grow shorter and darker, and the winter solstice when the days begin to grow longer and brighter.

In ancient times a plentiful supply of food depended on the weather. There were no shops back then; people had to grow enough food to feed themselves. They also had to store sufficient food for the winter when no crops could be grown, so knowledge of the seasons was of immense importance. They had to know when was the best time to sow seeds, when to gather the crops and when to start preserving food for the winter.

There were no fridges or freezers in those times either, so preserving food was vital. Meat would have been smoked and dried to preserve it. Edible roots would be preserved in pits covered with earth. Fungi and other edible roots would be dried and hung up in a cool, dark place. When I was growing up on a small farm, we still used these methods of preserving meat and vegetables over the winter.

The winter, as you know, is a dark, cold time with the days getting colder and darker until the winter solstice on 21 December. From then on, the days begin to grow longer and warmer, with the promise of spring. So 21 December was a very important day for those ancient Irish people. On that day they would have held religious ceremonies to give thanks to their gods that they had survived the dark winter and could now look forward to the coming spring. They would also have had great celebrations with feasting and music and dancing.

Can you imagine one of those religious ceremonies and celebrations? First, a great fire is lit to give both light and heat. The whole tribe, men, women and children then gather in a ring around the fire. Drums begin to beat and the druids dance around the blazing fire, the leaping flames casting their shadows on the glowing faces of those watching them. The druids are probably naked, their bodies dyed with woad, a blue dye obtained from a plant. They begin to chant, their voices echoing out in the darkness beyond the fire's glow. Others begin to play whistles and then bronze horns are sounded, like the deep baying of some gigantic animal.

The druids' dance becomes more frenzied and their chanting grows louder. Bigger drums begin to boom and mingled with all those sounds is the droning of the horns. The druids are offering prayers to the gods in thanksgiving for the bountiful supply of food and for the continued good health of the people. They are asking the gods to grant them good weather when spring comes so that their people can plant their seeds. They pray, too, for a bumper crop at harvest time so that the tribe will again have sufficient food for the winter.

Now the druids offer up a sacrifice to the gods. An animal is killed and its blood sprinkled on the earth, or even on the people gathered around the fire. A terrible thing – something we would not want to think about too much – is that sometimes a human sacrifice was made to the gods. Two male bodies, known as Clonycavan Man and Old Croghan Man, were found preserved in bogs in recent times. Both are thought to have been sacrificed to the gods. I'm glad to say that these sacrifices only took place on rare occasions, maybe when a new chief took over leadership of the tribe. The druids also buried valuable objects, or threw them into lakes as offerings to the gods. This is why we have found so many of these objects, which have helped us to understand our ancestors and their beliefs and how they lived.

Because the people believed that the druids could persuade the gods to send sunshine or rain as required, they were revered and regarded with awe. Even the chiefs of the community feared and respected them. The chiefs would consult the druids before making any major decision, and so those men possessed great powers and privileges within their communities. Another group who held great power and privilege was the poets, or *fili* in Gaelic. They kept alive the stories and traditions and history of the people, and were held in great esteem.

The arrival of the Celts changed Ireland forever. It became a Celtic nation and within 500 years the Celtic language, religion and customs were a normal part of everyday life. But warfare between different tribes also became a part of Irish life, and this violence brought great changes to the way people lived.

7
The Coming of Kings

When the first people came to Ireland they would have belonged to one family or tribe. One man would have been the leader and would have made all the important decisions. If he had a son, then he became the leader when his father got too old or died. As the family got bigger, that leader gained more power. He now had more people to look after and to make decisions for.

If a tribe was attacked and conquered then the members of that tribe became slaves for their conquerors. This gave the conquerors even more power, for now they had men, women and even children to work on their behalf. They could produce more food and goods, which they could then swap for things they needed. This swapping of goods is called barter. There was no money back then and so people had to barter what they possessed for what they needed. If a tribe had access to copper and tin and was good at making bronze axes, they could barter them with a tribe who made objects from leather, or that made pottery.

When the Celts arrived, they were more powerful than the people already living in Ireland. They conquered these native people and became richer and even more powerful. As they grew more and more powerful, so did their leaders and their families, along with the druids and the *filí*. They lived in the biggest and best houses, had the best food and drink served to them by slaves, and wore the best clothes and gold ornaments.

But where there are rich and powerful tribes there are also problems. Other tribes become envious and wish to conqueror their neighbours and take all that power and wealth for themselves. Before the Celts came to Ireland, there was fighting and conquering occurring among the tribes already living here. With the arrival of the Celts, this conquering increased. Communities were forced to protect themselves and this is one reason why they built hill forts and raths and cashels.

Within his fortress, the tribal leader and his people could live in relative safety while protecting their animals and food and property from marauders. From here, the chief could rule over the other tribes around him who were not as powerful as he was. Gradually these chiefs became kings of their areas and eventually five major areas, or kingdoms emerged. These were the four provinces we still know today along with that of Meath. When we now refer to one of the four provinces in Gaelic we use the word '*cuige*'. Cuig means 'five' in Gaelic and refers back to that time when there were five provinces.

Later still, Ireland was divided into seven areas or kingdoms. Each of these kingdoms had its own king. These areas were then divided into smaller areas called tuaths and these, too, had their own king. There was constant warfare between these kings, and sometimes forts were not sufficient to protect one area from another. You remember, there was no money back then, and a king's wealth was measured in the number of cattle he possessed. So when kings went to war they would also try to steal the other king's cattle.

When war broke out between Connacht and Ulster, the Ulster people built giant earthworks to separate the two areas. These would have helped to protect them from the attackers, and prevented the attackers from stealing cattle. A section of these earthworks, known as Black Pig's Dyke, still exists today. The name, according to legend, is associated with a magician who was tricked into becoming a pig, and was then forced to travel around Ireland rooting up the earth into gigantic banks.

Of course, this is just a legend, but as there are many such earthworks around the country, this indicates that there was much warfare. Some kings became very powerful and wished to be High King of all Ireland, or *Ard Rí* in Gaelic. But though many claimed to be High King, in reality there was no one king who ruled all of Ireland at this time.

Still, there were some very powerful kings in Ireland living in magnificent forts. One of the most famous of all these Irish forts was Emain Macha, or Navan fort. It was in Armagh, and was founded either by a Queen Macha, or was called after a goddess of that name. It later became the residence of one of Ireland's most famous kings, Conor Mac Nessa, who reigned in Ulster about 2,000 years ago. It was at his court that the great hero Cú Chulainn lived. The Red Branch Knights, who were brave warriors, also lived at Navan fort.

The kings of Connacht lived at Rathcroghan, County Roscommon, the kings of Leinster at Dún Ailinne, County Kildare, and the kings of Munster at Cashel, County Tipperary. But the most famous of all Irish forts was the great fort on the hill of Tara, in County Meath. Its origins date back to Stone Age times, when there was a settlement there. One of its most famous kings was Cormac Mac Airt, who was the son of Art and the grandson of a king named Conn, who gave his name to Connacht. During his reign, Cormac Mac Airt made Tara the capital of Ireland. He lived there in a magnificent palace and within the fort was a great banqueting hall, said to be the largest building in all of Ireland.

According to legend, Cormac founded the Fianna, whose leader was Fionn MacCumhaill. He was a great warrior and lived on the nearby Hill of Allen. The Fianna could be said to be Ireland's first army, and many stories are told of their brave deeds. However, it is difficult to know what is actually true and what is legend. But they make great stories; so much so that they are still related today, part of our folklore and myth. Legend claims that the Fianna became too powerful and were defeated in a great battle at Gavra, County Meath, by Cormac's grandson, Cairbre.

For hundreds of years, Tara was the most important fort in the country and whoever ruled there was virtually the High King. There was a stone there called the *Lia Fáil*, or Stone of Destiny, and when the rightful king touched it, it cried out. This part about the stone crying out is clearly a myth, but perhaps a druid cried out and this gave rise to the legend. The stone can still be seen at Tara today.

The king who ruled at Tara was so powerful that every third year a great gathering, the Feis of Tara, was held, to which were invited the other Irish kings. At this gathering, the kings would discuss making new laws, which were known as the Brehon Laws, 'Brehon' being the Gaelic word for judge. After this, and when the weaker kings had paid honour to the more powerful ones, a great feast, known as the Feast of Tara was held. During this time athletic contests and games took place, and there was much music and song and story, and of course feasting on the best food and drink. The feast lasted for three whole days, though it's claimed that it could go on for weeks or months.

Yet despite these great gatherings of the Irish kings, disputes between different kings continued. Alliances were formed and broken and war could be waged for wrongs done, or for even imagined wrongs. Stories about many of these disputes were later written down. One of the most famous is The Cattle-Raid of Cooley. This tells the story of the war between Queen Maeve of Connacht and Conor Mac Nessa of Ulster. Maeve invaded Ulster in a dispute over the ownership of the brown bull of Cooley. Cú Chulainn, one of Ireland's most famous mythical heroes, also appears in this story and was killed in the fighting. Maeve was victorious, and her victory probably marked the beginning of the decline of Navan fort and the power of the Ulster kings.

This story about Queen Maeve is interesting for two reasons. Again it shows the importance of cattle to the Irish at that time. In an economy based on ownership of cattle, a fine bull was a very valuable animal indeed and well worth going to war over. It also shows that not all the leaders in Ireland were men.

Around 1,000 years after the Celts first came to Ireland this was what life in the country was like. The people were mostly farmers ruled over by kings who lived in forts or raths or cashels, and who in turn owed allegiance to other kings. The people were pagans and worshipped their gods with the help of the druids. From time to time warriors came from across the seas to raid along the Irish coast. Meanwhile, the Irish carried out raids on the coasts of Britain. One group of Irish people from Ulster went to live in Scotland, in a place now known as Argyll. It was they who made Scotland a Gaelic nation and today both countries have much in common, including music and dance and language.

Around the year AD 400, the king at Tara was known as Niall of the Nine Hostages because he took hostages from his enemies so that they would not attack him. He is regarded as one of the greatest of all Irish kings, and one who could lay some claim to being a real High King. He was a warlike king, tall and fair haired with intense blue eyes. He often raided the coast of Britain and even went as far as France, where, it is claimed, he was eventually killed during a raid.

On one of his raids along the British coast, probably the coast of what we now call Wales, he captured 200 slaves and brought them back to Ireland. Among them was a young boy of Roman descent who was about sixteen years of age. Unknown to Niall or his warriors, or even to the boy himself, it was to be a momentous event for Ireland. For that young boy was later destined to utterly change the course of Ireland's history.

8
Saint Patrick

Icannot tell you the history of Ireland, and of the effect that young boy had on our country, without sometimes looking at the history of the world. During those first 7,000 years of Irish history, great empires rose and fell elsewhere in the world. One of these empires was that of the Egyptians, who built the pyramids. Another empire was that of the Romans, who got their name from Rome, which was one of the greatest cities on earth for about 1,000 years.

Legend claims that the city of Rome was founded around 2,700 years ago by twin boys named Romulus and Remus, who were reared by wolves. Unfortunately, the twins quarrelled, and Romulus killed his brother and named the city after himself. Although we cannot prove that any of this is true, we do know that Rome governed the most powerful empire on earth for about 1,000 years.

The Romans had a magnificent army with highly trained soldiers, and they conquered most of the lands around the Mediterranean Sea. They also conquered Britain, except for Scotland. Fierce warriors known as Scots and Picts lived there, and the Romans could not defeat them. These Scots and Picts constantly attacked the Romans and this forced them to build a great wall dividing England from Scotland, just as the men of Ulster had built Black Pig's Dyke. The emperor who built this wall was called Hadrian and you can still see part of Hadrian's Wall today.

Now, a question that is often asked is: did the Romans try to conquer Ireland? There is some evidence that Agricola, who was governor of Britain around the year AD 80, planned to invade Ireland. But trouble with the Scots prevented him from doing so. There is also evidence that the Romans had a fort near Dublin and some historians believe that they may have founded the original settlement at Cashel, County Tipperary.

Roman coins and arms and other Roman objects have been found in Ireland. But Ireland is so close to Britain that it would be strange if these did not find their way here. We know Irish kings raided the British coast and must have taken coins and arms and goods back home with them. The Romans were great seafarers and it seems certain that they must have visited Ireland just out of curiosity. But there is no evidence of a large scale invasion. The Romans were renowned as builders of towns and roads and aqueducts and had they conquered Ireland, they would have built some of these and their remains would still be here.

The Romans were pagans and worshipped many gods. But following the death of Jesus Christ in AD 33, many people in the Roman world became Christians. The Roman emperors persecuted them and many were martyred. Then around the year AD 300, a man named Constantine became Roman emperor. His mother, Helena, was a Christian and because of this, her son did not persecute Christians. Legend tells us that one day, while he was leading his men in battle, he saw a cross appear in the sky. Constantine was victorious in the battle and he took this as a sign that Christianity was the true religion. From then on he decreed that it would be the religion of the Roman Empire. As a result of this, Christianity came to Britain.

By the year AD 400 the Romans had withdrawn their armies from Britain to defend Rome and their empire from people called the Visigoths and Vandals. The Vandals sacked Rome in AD 455 and even today, if someone destroys property, or paints graffiti on a building, we say they are a vandal. With the sacking of Rome, the Roman Empire fell. Europe was plunged into a period we know as the Dark Ages, which lasted for about 1,000 years. During this time wars raged in Europe as different peoples tried to gain land and power for themselves.

However, the first 400 years of the Dark Ages were a Golden Age for Ireland. During this time, learning became very important and magnificent books were written and wonderful objects were made from gold and silver. Yet this Golden Age began with violence when Niall of the Nine Hostages captured those 200 slaves, including that sixteen-year-old boy. His name was Patrick, and today Patrick is one of the most famous and revered of all Irish Christian names.

The terrified boy was brought to Ireland in chains and sold to a farmer named Miliuc in County Antrim. Here, Patrick was forced to tend a herd of sheep and pigs on Slemish Mountain for six years. In a letter of his which survives, he writes in Latin that he spent his time in prayer and that one day he heard a voice telling him that a ship was waiting to take him home.

Patrick ran away and eventually reached the coast, probably at Wicklow. Here, he found a ship but the captain would not take him on board. Patrick stowed away on the ship and eventually he made his way home to Britain. Once there, he decided to become a priest. After he was ordained, he claimed to have heard the voices of the people of Ireland begging him to return and convert them to Christianity.

The Pope gave Patrick permission to travel to Ireland and he arrived here at a time that we now know as Easter in the year 432. Ireland was still a pagan country, though some of the people were Christians. They had been converted by a bishop called Palladius, who had earlier been sent to Ireland by the Pope.

One of the pagan ceremonies that took place in Ireland at this time of year was the lighting of a great fire on the Hill of Tara by Laoghaire, who was the king who lived in the royal fort at this time. This fire was lit at the spring equinox, that important day in the calendar which is divided equally between twelve hours of daylight and twelve hours of darkness. Until the king lit this fire, no one else could dare light any other fire.

Legend tells us that Patrick, and those who were with him, built a great pile of wood on the Hill of Slane, which is visible from Tara. Patrick then lit this fire before the king lit his and it was seen by all at Tara. Laoghaire was furious and he gathered his soldiers and rode to the Hill of Slane, intent on killing whoever had defied him. The king and his soldiers galloped to the top of the hill only to be met by Patrick and his unarmed followers. They were unafraid, and their courage impressed the king. Instead of killing them all, Laoghaire demanded to know who they were and what they were doing.

Patrick began to preach the Christian message and this, too, impressed the king. It is said that Patrick used the shamrock to explain the mystery of three persons in one God to the king. As you know, the shamrock is one of the emblems of Ireland, and we wear shamrock on Saint Patrick's Day to honour the man who first brought Christianity to Ireland, and who is also our patron saint.

Laoghaire did not kill Patrick or his followers, nor did he himself convert to Christianity. Instead, he gave Patrick permission to go about the country preaching Christianity and converting the people. Patrick did so, though it wasn't easy. Not everyone was as understanding as Laoghaire and the druids especially did not wish to see their pagan religion replaced. If that happened, they would lose all their power and influence. Often on his travels, Patrick and his followers were in grave danger, and at times were imprisoned. However, such was Patrick's courage and his faith, that he always persuaded those who persecuted him to let him live and continue his preaching and converting.

Because of his travels, many places in Ireland are associated with him and bear his name. Some of these are Croagh Patrick, where he is supposed to have stayed for forty days and nights, fasting and praying, and Downpatrick Head, both of which are in County Mayo. He is also supposed to have visited Saint Patrick's Purgatory, which is on an island in Lough Derg, County Donegal, and Downpatrick in County Down, where he is allegedly buried. Some historians claim that Patrick went to France and died and was buried there.

Armagh is also closely associated with Patrick because he founded the most important Irish church there. It still remains the most important church in Ireland today. We don't know exactly when Patrick died, but it is thought that he lived for thirty years after he came to Ireland and died on 17 March, which is now his feast day, in 462.

There are many legends associated with Saint Patrick. One of the most famous is that he banished the snakes from Ireland. The legend claims that one snake refused to be banished so Patrick made a box and ordered the snake into it. The snake claimed that the box was too small and an argument ensued between the two. Patrick persuaded the snake to prove that the box was too small by slithering into it. Having tricked the snake, Patrick closed the box, trapping it inside. He then threw the box into the sea, into which he had already driven all the other snakes. We don't really believe this legend; yet there are no snakes in Ireland today.

What is true about Patrick is that he was one of the most important men ever to come to Ireland. Not only did he bring Christianity, but with that faith came writing and learning, and the start of what we call the Golden Age. While wars raged in Europe, and tribes called Angles and Saxons conquered England, Ireland became a land of 'saints and scholars'.

9
Monasteries and Missionaries

Before Saint Patrick came to Ireland, the only form of writing in the country was a simple Celtic script known as ogham. This consisted of groups of marks, like dashes, with each group representing a letter of the alphabet. With this system of writing, simple words like a person's name could be cut on the edge of a stone. But with the coming of Saint Patrick and Christianity, Latin, the language of the Romans, came to Ireland. The oldest pieces of writing in Latin to survive from that time are two letters written by Saint Patrick himself.

The coming of Saint Patrick utterly changed the way of life in Ireland over the next few hundred years. As Christianity spread throughout the country, a great many monasteries were founded. Some of the most important of these were at Clonard, County Meath; Clonfert, County Galway; Clonmacnoise, County Offaly; Durrow, County Laois; Glendalough, County Wicklow; and Derry, beside the River Foyle. At first, these monasteries were comprised of a wooden church along with accommodation for the monks. Later, these wooden buildings were replaced with stone buildings. There were also workshops and granaries and bakeries and kitchens and schools and rooms where monks wrote and copied manuscripts, and where they could study. There were also hospitals where the sick were cared for.

The monks who lived in the monasteries were engaged in numerous tasks. They made beautiful religious objects in gold and silver, set with jewels. These were chalices and patens and crosses, which were used in celebrating Mass. They also made reliquaries, which are boxes to hold relics of saints, and high crosses from carved stone. Two of the most beautiful objects dating from this time are the Ardagh and Derrynaflan chalices.

Monasteries and Missionaries

The monks also made elaborate boxes, called cumdachs, in which to store the books they wrote. Books were very important and valuable in those days, and were all written by hand. They were not written on paper but on vellum, which is made from the skins of animals, usually calves, sheep and goats. The inks were made from plants like saffron, turmeric and woad; from earth, like yellow ochre; and from charcoal or burned bones and even from insects. Urine and earwax were also used in making up the inks, which doesn't sound very pleasant at all.

These books, or to give them their correct title, manuscripts (because they were written by hand), were in Latin. They were decorated with religious paintings and highly intricate drawings in vivid colours. When you looked at a page it seemed as if a light glowed behind it, and this is why they are described as 'illuminated'. Did you know that the largest surviving collection of European manuscripts from those times comes from Ireland?

Two of the most famous of these illuminated manuscripts are The Book of Durrow and The Book of Kells, both of which are in Trinity College in Dublin. The Book of Durrow, containing the four gospels, was probably written in the late seventh or early eighth century, and is the oldest surviving Irish illuminated manuscript. The Book of Kells, which also contains the four gospels, was probably written sometime in the ninth century. Some historians believe it was written on the island of Iona, off the Scottish coast. It is regarded as one of the finest illuminated manuscripts in the world.

During the Golden Age, Latin was the written language. Later, many of the old stories and myths and legends of Ireland began to be written down in Gaelic for the first time and it then became a written, as well as a spoken, language. The oldest surviving manuscript in Gaelic is The Book of the Dun Cow, which was probably written in the eleventh century. It contains many of the old myths and legends, including the story of The Cattle Raid of Cooley.

There were no printing presses or computers back then, so manuscripts had to be copied word for word by hand using quills and ink. The monks who did this were called scribes and often the only light they had was from candles or oil lamps. Sometimes they worked for years writing or copying a single book, and no doubt their fingers were permanently stained with ink.

One man who was involved in copying manuscripts was Columcille, who is now a saint. Whenever he copied a manuscript, he kept the copy for himself. Once, Columcille copied a book belonging to Saint Finian and kept the copy for himself. Finian was angry at this and complained about it to the High King, Diarmuid, and asked him to decide who owned the copy.

Diarmuid gave a famous judgement, based on one of the Brehon Laws, which you remember were the laws in force in Ireland at that time. This law stated that a calf that wandered away from a farm always belonged to its mother. If the calf wandered onto another farm the farmer could not claim that it belonged to him. Now the High King declared: 'To every cow its calf and to every book its copy.' So Columcille couldn't keep the copy of the book. Today we call this law copyright, and no one can copy a book without the permission of the person who owns the copyright.

Some of our most famous Irish saints also lived during those times. The best known of them are Saint Finian, Saint Kevin, Saint Columbanus, Saint Brendan, Saint Ciaran, Saint Columcille and Saint Brigid, who is almost as important a saint in Ireland today as Saint Patrick. She was born around 453 at Faughart, County Louth, the daughter of a local chieftain. When she grew up she decided to devote her life to God. She founded a convent and built her church beneath an oak tree. In Gaelic, this church was called '*Cill Dara*', the church of the oak, or as we know it today in English, Kildare.

Just as with Saint Patrick, there is a legend associated with Saint Brigid. It is said that when she wished to found her convent she asked the local king for land on which to build it. He said that he would give her as much land as her cloak would cover. This amount, of course, would be tiny. But legend says that Saint Brigid placed her cloak on the ground and that it spread out until it covered an enormous amount of land. The king was so impressed – or more likely terrified – at seeing this, that he granted Saint Brigid the land.

Monasteries and Missionaries

Her feast day is celebrated on 1 February and on that day many schoolchildren in Ireland make a Saint Brigid's Cross from green rushes. Another legend tells us that Saint Brigid made the cross from rushes while she was trying to convert a dying pagan chieftain. It's claimed that when she had made the cross and showed it to the chieftain he converted to Christianity.

But while many of these Irish saints remained in Ireland, others left to preach the gospel in Scotland and England and in France and Germany and elsewhere in Europe. It is claimed that Saint Brendan, who was known as The Navigator because he made so many sea voyages, actually sailed to America almost 1,000 years before Christopher Columbus. We don't know if this is true, but Saint Brendan did sail to the islands of Scotland and to England preaching the gospel. Irish missionaries were so successful in England that for over 100 years the kings of Northumbria spoke Irish.

Saint Columcille was another man who travelled from Ireland to preach the gospel. He was born into an important family in Garten, County Donegal, in 521 and founded a great monastery at Derry. Later, when he travelled out of Ireland to preach the gospel, he did so for a different reason from other missionaries. You remember how Diarmuid gave his famous judgement, 'to every book its copy?' At first, Columcille did not accept this judgement, and he raised an army to fight Diarmuid. There was a great battle at Cúl Drebene in Sligo in which 2,000 men died. Columcille was so horrified at this slaughter, which he had caused, that he determined to travel away from Ireland and convert 2,000 pagans to Christianity. He sailed to the island of Iona off the Scottish coast and founded a famous monastery there.

Saint Columbanus, who was born in Leinster probably around 550, is another famous Irish missionary. He, along with twelve other monks, sailed to France where they founded a monastery. At a time when Europe was ravaged by wars between different tribes, this monastery was a haven of peace and learning. Columbanus also travelled through Switzerland and on to Italy where he founded another monastery at Bobbio. He died there in 615.

Other Irish missionaries went to Germany, which was a very dangerous place at this time. The Visigoths, the Vandals and another tribe of people, the Huns, were constantly fighting for supremacy. The Visigoths were successful, but they were then attacked around 750 by Arabs and Berbers who came from the east. Despite this constant warfare, the Irish missionaries founded monasteries there which also became centres of learning. It is claimed that these monasteries kept learning alive in Europe during the Dark Ages. Because of the influence of these Irish missionaries in Europe, many people from there came to Ireland to be educated at our monasteries and this too helped to keep learning alive outside Ireland.

But not all these holy Irishmen lived in large monasteries, or travelled abroad. Many became hermits, or lived in small groups in lonely, uninhabited places. One of the most famous of those places is the hermitage on Skellig Michael, which is little more than a large rock off the coast of Kerry. Here, with flat stones, the monks built huts, resembling beehives, and lived simple lives of poverty, fasting and prayer.

Of course, Ireland wasn't totally at peace during those times, but compared to Britain and Europe, it was a haven of tranquillity. Wars were still fought between different kings as they sought power for themselves. Over the 400 or so years of the Golden Age, new families, or clans, emerged as the most powerful and important in the country. The most famous and powerful of these were the O'Neills of Ulster, the O'Briens of Munster and the O'Connors of Connacht, all of whom would play major parts in the future history of Ireland.

We said earlier that whoever ruled at Tara claimed to be High King of Ireland. Though he did have great power, he didn't really control the whole country. As other families, or clans, became more powerful, the power and influence of the king of Tara waned. Eventually, the great fortress became uninhabited and reverted to the green grassy hill it once had been, just as had happened to Navan fort in Armagh. If history teaches us anything, it is that the powerful eventually fall, and even great empires crumble to dust and that nothing, not even a Golden Age, lasts forever.

Monasteries and Missionaries

After 400 or so years of the Golden Age, dark clouds began to gather over Ireland. A storm was approaching the shores, but this was not a storm of nature. This was a storm of men and it brought fierce, brutal warriors from Scandinavia to plunder the monasteries and to kill anyone who dared oppose them. These men were known as the Vikings, and were some of the most feared warriors ever to invade Ireland. Like the young boy, Patrick, they too were destined to change the course of Irish history: this time not with the gospel, but with killing and bloodshed.

10
The Vikings

It must have been a terrifying sight to see a Viking raiding party coming ashore from their longboats. These boats were not like the Irish boats, which were made of timber frames covered in animal skins. The longboats, up to 20 metres in length, were built of overlapping oak planks and could carry 100 men. They were propelled by oars and by a sail, and had gigantic carved prows, which often depicted the head of a terrifying imaginary creature like a dragon.

The Viking men were big and burly and dressed in rough breeches and tunics made of wool or leather and woollen cloaks. They wore helmets, which were much like iron bowls turned upside down. A piece of metal hung down at the front to protect the nose. Today, these helmets are usually depicted as having had horns at either side, rather like the horns of a cow or goat. Historians now believe that they did not have such horns. But the warriors must have still looked menacing, and this impression would have been enhanced by the fact that most of them would have had great shaggy beards and long unruly hair. They would have been screaming and beating their swords against their shields as they carried out their raids.

They were very well armed with spears and swords and battleaxes and also with bows and arrows. All warriors carried a shield made of wood with a leather cover, and these shields were hung along the sides of the boat while they were at sea. If they were attacked, they could raise the shields to form a barrier from behind which they could fight their enemy. Only the most important of the warriors had swords, and these were highly decorated and carried in wooden scabbards, which were then hung from their waists by leather thongs. The Vikings were very proud

The Vikings

of their swords and actually gave them names, like Leg-biter. This name might seem amusing, but it would not have been at all funny if your leg was 'bitten off' by a slash from this sword. The Vikings themselves also had nicknames, like Flat Nose, Hairy Breeks, Belly Shaker and Skull Splitter. Again, they might seem amusing, but don't you wonder how Skull Splitter got his name? I certainly wouldn't wish to meet him!

The Vikings came from Norway, Sweden and Denmark and were pagans. Many of them were farmers and fishermen and only went raiding other countries in their spare time. They were magnificent seafarers and one of them, Eric the Red, is supposed to have sailed to America in about the year 1000. The Vikings not only raided the coast of Ireland, but also the coasts of Britain, France, Germany and other parts of Europe. Like the Irish raiders of earlier times, they were seeking food and goods and valuable objects made of precious metals and slaves.

When they first attacked Ireland around AD 795, they only raided along the coast. They came quickly and without warning from the sea, attacked a monastery or a settlement, and withdrew again as quickly as they had come, taking their booty and slaves with them. Later, because their boats were light and easy to manoeuvre, they began to raid inland, travelling deep into the country by river.

At first, the Irish had no answer to these raiders. Those who lived in the monasteries were holy, peaceful men and not warriors. They were easily overcome, though not without a great deal of bloodshed, for the Vikings were bloodthirsty, and even killed people who posed them no threat.

As the number of raids increased, the monks took action to protect themselves. Whenever there was the threat of an attack, they hid their most valued treasures, usually by burying them. This is why from time to time we have found this buried treasure. In these circumstances, we have to assume that no one was left behind in the monastery to dig up the treasure once the Vikings left. So everyone must have been killed or taken as slaves.

The monks also built round towers, tall circular buildings, which also doubled as bell towers, the bell being rung to warn of a raid. These towers, which can still be seen dotted about the Irish countryside, could have up to five floors, which were reached by ladders inside the tower. The most important point about these towers was that the only entrance was situated high up on the wall and could only be reached by a ladder, which then could be pulled up once everyone was inside.

The ringing of the bell must have struck terror into everyone who heard it. All knew that they had to gain the safety of the round tower before the bloodthirsty warriors arrived. Everyone in the monastery and the surrounding area would have stopped what they were doing and rushed to the tower. There would have been great panic and much screaming and crying. In the distance, the terror-stricken people would have heard the more terrifying screams and shouts and the beating of weapons on shields of the approaching raiders.

Amidst great confusion, the people would have scrambled up the ladder and into the tower. Once everyone was inside, the ladder was drawn up and the entrance closed off by a heavy wooden door. The people inside were now safe from attack and from narrow slits in the walls could defend themselves. They may have been able to throw spears at the Vikings or shoot arrows at them or throw stones down on top of them. But they could not prevent the plundering and burning that went on, and could only look on helplessly until the raiders had taken whatever was of value and returned to their ships, leaving buildings and crops in flames.

After years of carrying out raids on Ireland, the Vikings changed their tactics. Instead of returning home after a raid, they remained behind, at first settling along the coast. They founded settlements in Dublin, Wexford, Waterford, Cork and Limerick, and these settlements eventually became towns and great centres of trade. Within fifty years of their first raids, a Viking, Olaf the White, ruled Dublin. When he was killed, Ivar the Boneless, son of Ragnar Hairy-Britches, became king.

During this time the Vikings continued to fight the native Irish and to raid monasteries and other settlements. Then, like the Celts before them, they began to mingle with the Irish population. Marriages took place between the Vikings and the Irish. Alliances were also formed and often the Vikings and an Irish king would join forces to wage war on another Irish king or even on other Vikings. One great battle was fought at Tara in 980 in which Malachy II, king of Meath and who claimed to be the High King, defeated the Vikings and their Irish allies. Malachy also defeated and captured another Viking warrior, Turgeis. He had Turgeis placed in a barrel, which was then rolled down a hill into Lough Ennell, County Westmeath, where the Viking leader drowned.

At this time, there was still no real High King of Ireland, though many kings, like Malachy II, laid claim to such a title. Then around the year 1000 a man emerged who could rightly claim to be the High King of Ireland. His name was Brian Boru, and he was already king of the O'Briens of Munster.

Brian Boru was born around AD 940 and lived at the O'Briens fort at Kincora, near Killaloe, County Clare. He defeated the Vikings and his Irish enemies in many battles, and threatened to make war on Malachy II to ensure the High King's title for himself. Malachy, not wishing to make war, yielded, and Brian Boru became the first real High King of Ireland in 1002.

Brian was a good High King and wished to rid the country of the Vikings. In the year 1014, he gathered a large army and marched on Dublin, which was the chief Viking town in Ireland. At Clontarf, on Good Friday, 23 April 1014, Brian's men met an army of Vikings and their Irish allies from Leinster. The fierce battle, the largest fought in Ireland up to that time, raged all day. Brian's army triumphed and facing defeat, the Vikings tried to flee to their ships. However, many were drowned as the tide came in and trapped them.

By now, Brian Boru was an old man and did not take part in the battle. Instead, he stayed in his royal tent praying for victory. A fleeing Viking, Brodar, king of the Isle of Man, burst into Brian's tent and slew him with one blow of his battleaxe before he himself was killed by Brian's men.

While the Battle of Clontarf forever broke the power of the Vikings in Ireland, Brian's death left the position of High King in a weakened state. Almost 150 years would pass, along with much fighting among the different clans, before another man could claim to be High King of all Ireland.

But though the Vikings had been defeated, all of them did not leave Ireland. Instead, they remained, mostly in the towns. They introduced the use of money, and Dublin was the first Irish town to use coins. The towns along the coast continued trading with Britain and the continent, and as a result they grew bigger and became important centres where trades and crafts were carried out. Dublin (in Gaelic *Dubh Linn*, the 'black pool') was the most important of all the towns. From the time of the Vikings it became the capital of Ireland.

The Vikings who remained in Ireland and the native Irish continued to merge, especially in the towns, while the various kings continued fighting among themselves. Each king desired to be High King and over the next 150 years one king or another tried to claim the title. Eventually, about1150, the O'Connors of Connacht emerged as the most powerful clan in the country. Their leader was Rory O'Connor, and by 1169 he could rightly claim to be High King. But what he or his followers, or indeed anyone else in Ireland could not have known was that Rory was destined to be the last High King of Ireland. For another dark storm was brewing over the country, a storm of wars and bloodshed that was to make the Viking wars seem insignificant in comparison.

A new enemy, much stronger and more dangerous than the Vikings, was about to invade Ireland. This enemy would not be so easily defeated and was destined to plunge Ireland into centuries of wars, rebellions, hardship and bloodshed. The dispute that led to the invasion began, as many such disputes do, over the minor matter of who should be king of Leinster. But it persisted for 800 years over the more important matter of who should be king of Ireland.

11
The Normans

Once again we must look at the history of other countries in order to understand what happened in Ireland in 1169, and so we must go back to the year 1066. By then the Angles and Saxons had invaded and conquered England, and one of them, named Harold, was king. But he was not entitled to the throne.

The previous king of England had been Edward. He had been friendly with the people who lived in northern France, and who called themselves Normans. Many of them came to England to live at the Royal Court and Edward promised one of them, William, Duke of Normandy, that he could be king of England when Edward died.

The English people, now known as Anglo-Saxons, did not like the Normans, nor did they like Edward for inviting them to England. When Edward died, the people accepted Harold as their king. This angered William, and he became determined to invade England and claim the throne, which he had been promised by Edward.

In October 1066, William landed with a great army in the south of England. King Harold, with his army, marched to meet him. They met in a great battle at Hastings on Saturday 15 October 1066. Harold's army fought very bravely, but were defeated. Harold was killed at the end of the battle, one of only two English monarchs to die on the battlefield. Legend claims that he was accidentally shot through the eye by an arrow fired by one of his own men. He was the last Anglo-Saxon king of England and it was also the last time that England was conquered. William now declared himself king of England, and was crowned at Westminster on Christmas Day 1066. He fought many battles in France during his reign and was so successful at winning that he is known as William the Conqueror.

None of the Irish kings would have cared about this event, even if they had heard about it. At the time of the Battle of Hastings, they were, as usual, fighting among themselves over who should be High King to succeed Brian Boru, who had given himself the title Emperor of the Irish. Among those who wished to be High King were those from Brian's own tribe, the O'Briens, along with the O'Neills of Ulster and the O'Connors of Connacht. But none of them emerged as a recognised High King until the O'Connors of Connacht claimed that title. The most famous member of the family was Rory O'Connor, who became the last High King of Ireland in 1166.

When Rory became High King, trouble was already brewing. This trouble was caused by the king of Leinster, Dermot MacMurrough. He was an ambitious man and wanted to be High King. He was continually at war with his neighbouring kings, and his fiercest enemy was Tiernan O'Rourke, the one-eyed king of Breffni. In 1152 MacMurrough raided Breffni, stole cattle and abducted O'Rourke's wife, whom he held prisoner for a year. MacMurrough, though, claimed that she wished to leave her husband, and he had simply helped her. Whichever story is true, O'Rourke hated MacMurrough, and wanted revenge. His chance came in 1166.

By then MacMurrough's power had been weakened by constant fighting, and many of his supporters were dead. Aided by Rory O'Connor, O'Rourke and his allies marched against MacMurrough and defeated him in a number of battles. When his palace at Ferns in Wexford was captured, MacMurrough fled.

He sailed from Ireland to England to ask Henry II, who was then king of England, for help to regain his throne. Henry was away fighting in France and MacMurrough went there and met the king at Aquitane.

The Normans

Henry, like most kings, wanted more power and land, and had often considered conquering Ireland. But as his army was not large enough to fight in France and also invade Ireland, he had not done so. He didn't have any soldiers to loan to MacMurrough, but gave him permission to seek help from the Norman knights in Wales.

MacMurrough travelled to Wales where some Norman knights agreed to fight for him, one of whom was Richard Fitzgilbert de Clare. He was an expert with the longbow, a powerful weapon at the time, and was also known by the nickname 'Strongbow'. He had been the Earl of Pembroke, but had lost his lands when he took sides against King Henry II in one of the many disputes that arose over who should be king of England. Strongbow was anxious to regain land and power, and saw his opportunity. He was also an ambitious man who wanted to be a king in his own right. He made a bargain with Dermot that if he could marry Dermot's eldest daughter, Aoife, and become king of Leinster on Dermot's death, he would be willing to help.

Dermot, desperate to have revenge on his enemies and regain his kingdom, agreed to this. It was a terrible decision for Ireland and would lead to 800 years of strife in the country. Even yet the effects of that decision can be seen in the division of the country into the Republic of Ireland and Northern Ireland.

Dermot sailed for Ireland with some Norman knights, and at first had some success in battle. Eventually, Rory O'Connor and his allies defeated Dermot and his Norman knights, but now Rory made a serious mistake. Instead of driving Dermot and the Normans from Ireland, Rory forgave Dermot and allowed him to be king of part of Leinster. Dermot, instead of being thankful, became more determined to regain the whole of Leinster, and sought more help from the Normans in Wales. In May 1169, a Norman force landed at Bannow Bay, County Wexford. They marched on Wexford and captured the town. MacMurrough joined them, still determined to win back the kingship of all Leinster, but as yet he did not have enough men.

This problem was partly solved in the spring of 1170 when Raymond le Gros, landed in Waterford with a large Norman force. Strongbow then arrived in August 1170 with 200 Norman knights and 1,000 soldiers. Joined by MacMurrough's forces and those of Raymond le Gros, they marched on Waterford. The citizens fought bravely, but eventually the city was captured. Here, as promised, Strongbow married Dermot's daughter, Aoife, thus ensuring that the Norman knight would become king of Leinster when Dermot died.

The Normans were very good soldiers. The knights wore suits of chain-mail armour and iron helmets and carried great swords or maces. The armour was so heavy that they would not have been able to walk very well while wearing it, and so they rode horses, which were also protected with armour. They must have made a terrific din as they rode along with all that metal clinking and clanking. Accompanying them were archers on foot who were experts with longbows. The longbow was so powerful that its arrows could travel an enormous distance and still kill an enemy. It's said that when the archers released a shower of arrows you could hear them hiss as they flew threw the air, and that a shower of them could block out the sun. The Irish were not used to fighting such soldiers, which is why they were so quickly and easily defeated.

Strongbow, determined to secure his kingdom, now marched on Dublin, the most important Irish city. He captured the city, which was then in turn besieged by Rory O'Connor and his forces. After two months, Strongbow's forces rushed out and attacked the besiegers. Rory O'Connor was swimming in the River Liffey at the time, and was not expecting such an attack. He and his soldiers were caught by surprise and defeated. Strongbow now held all of Leinster and when Dermot MacMurrough died in 1171, Strongbow became king of Leinster. With his superior Norman knights to fight for him, he was now the most powerful man in Ireland.

This situation worried Henry II, who feared that Strongbow would become king of Ireland, and threaten his own rule in England. Henry decided to sail to Ireland and claim the country for himself. He landed in Waterford in October 1171 with an army so powerful that even Strongbow dared not oppose him. Instead, Strongbow and most Irish kings pledged loyalty to Henry, who now claimed Ireland as part of his

The Normans

kingdom, declaring himself Lord of Ireland. It was another momentous event in Irish history. Because of it, today, 850 years later, an English monarch still reigns over the six counties of Northern Ireland.

Before Henry II sailed from Ireland he granted some Irish lands to his Norman kinsfolk. This caused anger and resentment among those native Irish who lost their lands, and brought them into conflict with the Normans. Henry left John de Courcy in Ireland to conquer the northern part of the country, whose kings had not pledged loyalty to him. De Courcy marched north with his army and captured Downpatrick, the main Ulster stronghold. To defend the territory, he needed a secure base and built a Norman castle at Dundrum, County Down.

These first Norman castles were not built of stone. Instead, a wooden structure was built on a hilltop, or mound, called a motte. Here, the inhabitants could take shelter from their enemies. Below the mound a structure called a bailey was built. This was an area surrounded by a wooden palisade fence within which houses were built, and cattle and other animals and food and supplies kept safe.

Over the next 200 years the Normans captured more and more Irish land. Their success was often due to the fact that the Irish kings were always fighting among themselves. They even sided with the Normans against their own countrymen. Much of Leinster, Munster and Connacht came under Norman control. The Normans built great stone castles to defend their conquests and we can still see them today in the Irish countryside. These castles were built at Dublin, Kilkenny, Limerick, Carrickfergus in County Antrim, Trim in County Meath and at many other locations.

The Normans also developed the towns, which had been founded by the Vikings. Later they built great medieval cathedrals and introduced a number of religious orders to Ireland, like the Dominicans and the Franciscans. They also introduced the feudal system of land ownership, which was common in England and Europe. Under this system, the lord owned the land and protected the people who worked for him. They, in turn, owed complete allegiance to their master, and had to fight for him when necessary.

Over time, friendships and alliances were established between the conquerors and the native Irish. Marriages took place between both sets of people and the Normans began to adopt Irish habits and customs and language. This led to a saying that the Normans 'became more Irish than the Irish themselves'. They began to think of themselves as Irish, and felt that they no longer owed allegiance to an English king. This attitude brought English kings to Ireland from time to time, determined to assert their authority.

Gradually the Normans' real power base became centred in the eastern half of the country, especially around Dublin. They also controlled the main towns around the coast. Elsewhere, Irish kings, chieftains and Normans lived side by side, though as usual, there was a good deal of fighting among them, with alliances being formed and broken on a regular basis.

One of the most important points about the coming of the Normans to Ireland was that from then on the English monarchs claimed Ireland as part of their kingdom. But like the High Kings before them, they did not control the whole country. Yet this claim meant that Ireland's destiny was, from 1171 on, closely linked with that of England. Whenever there was a dispute in England over who should be the reigning monarch, it almost always affected Ireland. Battles for the English crown were later fought in Ireland, bringing great hardship on the people, including the descendants of the Normans. There were also many rebellions in Ireland to try and win her freedom from English rule, and for the next 800 years, Ireland was the scene of invasions, wars, rebellions, battles, sieges and famines, in which a great deal of blood was shed and tens of thousands of lives lost.

12
Robert the Bruce and the Spider

You will have realised by now that kings always want to conquer other lands and become even more powerful and rich. Henry II had declared himself Lord of Ireland, and the English kings who succeeded him wanted to be kings of Scotland and Wales as well. This led to wars between England and Wales, and England and Scotland, and one of these latter conflicts brought war to Ireland.

After they had conquered England, the Normans took lands in Wales. You remember Strongbow was a Norman whose family seized lands at Pembroke. But yet no English king could truly claim to be king of Wales. It was not until 1272, when Edward I was king of England, that Wales was conquered. Edward didn't like the Welsh or the Scots – he didn't like the Irish either – and was determined to conquer Wales and Scotland. In 1272 he led a great army into Wales, conquered the country and declared himself king. He now built massive castles and from these impregnable fortresses his soldiers could ensure that any rebellion was quickly subdued.

Edward knew that the Scots would not be as easily conquered as the Welsh. The Romans, who had conquered much of the then known world, had never conquered Scotland. So when Scottish king Alexander III died after falling from his horse, Edward I saw an opportunity for his own son to become king of Scotland.

Alexander's children had died before their father and his heir was his young granddaughter. Edward I arranged for his son to marry this girl, even though she was just six years of age. This would not have been a proper marriage, but still it would have been a terrible shock for the little girl. One day she's happily playing with her dolls and the next day she is to be married and a queen. But in olden times, arranged marriages between royal children were common as a king sought to ensure that his family would continue to rule after his death.

Unfortunately, this little girl died before she could marry. This, too, was quite common then. Even a simple illness could kill, as there were few medicines available to treat disease. When the child died, Edward nominated John Balliol to be king of Scotland. He was a weak man, and was Edward's puppet. Under pressure from the Scots, who didn't like him, Balliol resigned. Edward was furious and he led his army into Scotland and in revenge murdered thousands of people in the town of Berwick.

This enraged the Scots, and one of them, William Wallace, rebelled against Edward, who now claimed to be king of Scotland. At first, Wallace was successful, but eventually he was defeated and executed by being hanged, drawn and quartered, not at all a pleasant way to die. After his death, Robert Bruce became the leader of the Scottish rebellion, but eventually was forced to flee Scotland. Legend claims that he took refuge in a cave on Rathlin Island off the coast of County Antrim, where he decided to give up his resistance to Edward. But then Bruce saw a spider trying to spin a web in a corner of the cave. Seven times the spider tried to spin the web and seven times it failed. At the eighth attempt it succeeded. This showed him that if you kept on trying you could succeed.

Bruce returned to Scotland and renewed his fight against the English. This time he was successful in battle and was crowned king of Scotland at Scone in 1306. Over the next eight years he captured most of the English-held castles in Scotland. Meanwhile, Edward I died and his son, Edward II, became king of England. He was enraged that Bruce should claim the Scottish crown, and in 1314, Edward marched north with the largest army ever seen in England. He was intent on defeating Bruce and declaring himself king of Scotland.

The Scottish and English armies met at Bannockburn, south of Stirling, on Sunday, 23 June 1314. The English numbered about 23,000 men, which included knights in armour and archers, while Bruce probably had about 9,000 men. He was greatly outnumbered, and seemed certain to be defeated.

But a famous incident before the battle gave the Scots great heart. An English knight, Henry de Bohun, spotted Bruce sitting on his horse. Bruce was not wearing armour and de Bohun charged him, certain that he could kill his enemy and cause the Scots to lose heart. An armoured knight charging at full gallop on a huge warhorse would have terrified any man. But Bruce was a brave man and instead of galloping to safety, he stood his ground. While his soldiers watched on in terror, certain that their leader was about to die, Bruce nimbly turned his own horse aside as de Bohun reached him. As the knight charged past, Bruce struck him on the head with his battleaxe, slicing through de Bohun's helmet and splitting his skull in two. Bruce's reaction was to complain that he had broken his battleaxe and ask for a new one.

The incident was seen as a good omen by the Scots and despite being outnumbered almost three to one, they won the battle which raged for two days. The English army was routed and Edward II fled for his life. Robert Bruce, or as he was more generally known, Robert the Bruce, was now the undisputed king of Scotland and reigned until his death in 1329.

Robert the Bruce had a brother, Edward, and after the victory at Bannockburn the brothers turned their attention to Ireland. They decided that a war there would weaken the English, who would have to send soldiers to Ireland to defend their territory. This could prevent the English from becoming strong enough to attack Scotland. The Scots had also been asked for help by the O'Neills and other Irish kings and chieftains, who were trying to keep their lands from being taken by the Normans and their Irish allies.

The Irish and Scots were closely linked. They had a common language and many Scots were of Irish descent, while many of the Irish in the north of Ireland had Scottish blood. You remember that Irishmen from the north had gone to Scotland and settled in Argyll. Some of them had become kings of Scotland. There were also links between the two countries because of the Irish missionaries like Columcille who had preached the gospel in Scotland. Soldiers from Scotland, called Gallowglasses, helped Irish kings fight the Normans. The Irish and Scots also disliked the English, whom they both saw as ruthless conquerors.

In May 1315, Edward Bruce landed near Larne, County Antrim with an army of 6,000 men. He was joined by O'Neill and other chieftains, and began to win back territory held by the English, but not without great slaughter and bloodshed. In June, at Carrickfergus, he was acknowledged by the Irish as King of Ireland, though in reality he never controlled more than the north-eastern part of Ireland.

Meanwhile in Connacht, encouraged by Bruce's success, the O'Connors, the descendants of Rory, rose up against the English. But they were defeated at the Battle of Athenry, where many of the O'Connors and other Irish kings were killed.

When Bruce and his army routed the English forces at the Battle of Kells, County Meath, Edward II decided to take decisive action. A large English army set out to engage Bruce in battle at Faughart, the birthplace of Saint Brigid, on 14 October 1318. Bruce was outnumbered and instead of waiting for reinforcements, decided to fight.

Bruce was killed in the battle and his army defeated. This defeat left Edward II still the undisputed Lord of Ireland and the opportunity for Ireland to win her freedom ended for now. But this was not the last battle to be fought on Irish soil over who should be king of Scotland or England. Ireland was still bound to England and within 150 years a war in England over who should be king, known as the War of the Roses, would affect Ireland.

But war did not bring the next great threat to Ireland and her people. Instead they were threatened by a more deadly foe – a tiny insect, which would cause more death and suffering that even that caused by the recent wars.

13
Black Death and the Wars of the Roses

The tiny insect, which brought such death to Ireland, was a flea. The disease it caused was called the plague, also known as the Black Death. It was transmitted to humans by fleas that lived on the blood of black rats. Almost everyone who came in contact with an infected person caught the disease, which meant it was at its worst in towns and cities. In Ireland, this affected the English settlers more than it did the Irish or the Normans, who lived mostly in rural areas.

The plague was widespread in Europe and by 1450 Europe's population had halved. Ireland did not fare any better, and the country virtually ground to a standstill. Trade ceased, crops were not sown or harvested, and people also died of starvation and other diseases. The worst effects of the plague ended within a year, but it continued to erupt from time to time over the next fifty years. Following the plague, many English landowners returned to England and fewer came to Ireland. The Irish, encouraged by Edward Bruce's campaign, had also won back some of their lands. By 1366, English control in Ireland had been greatly weakened.

At this time there were three distinct groups of people in Ireland. There were the native Irish, the descendants of the Celts; there were the Norman families, the descendants of those who had come with Strongbow and in the years since then, many of whom now thought of themselves as Irish; and there were the new English settlers who had been granted lands by English kings.

At the time of the plague, the Normans had been in Ireland for nearly 200 years. Over these two centuries many of them had begun to practise Irish customs, dress like the Irish, speak Irish and marry Irish men and women. They were, in the words of the famous quote, 'more Irish than the Irish themselves'. They, along with Irish kings, now controlled large areas of the country. The influence of the English was centred in an area around Dublin, which became known as the Pale. The new English settlers who lived there, and English settlers elsewhere in the country, no longer felt safe among the Irish and the Normans. They lived in fear of rebellion, of losing their lands and of being murdered. They were also alarmed that the Normans were now behaving like the Irish, and oftentimes siding with them in disputes against the English.

By 1366 Edward III was king of England and was alarmed at the situation in Ireland. He was so worried about losing control of Ireland that he sent his son, Lionel, to be his representative in the country. This position has been known by many names and so as not to confuse you, I'm going to call it the Viceroy. Lionel summoned a parliament, consisting of English settlers from the Pale, in Kilkenny in November 1366. This parliament passed laws, which are known as the Statutes of Kilkenny. These laws forbade the Normans and the English settlers from wearing native Irish clothes, practising Irish customs, playing Irish games like hurling, speaking Irish or marrying Irish persons. However, the Normans ignored them, which continued to alarm the settlers in the Pale and the English king.

In 1377, Richard II became king of England. He was then only ten years old and his uncle, John of Gaunt, ruled the country. When Richard was old enough to rule, he decided to regain control of Ireland. In October 1394 he landed at Waterford with a great army of 34,000 men. His campaign seemed a success when many Irish kings publicly submitted to him. But once he returned to England the Irish kings continued on as before.

Richard, like most kings, made many enemies in England, and on his return from Ireland he had some of these enemies murdered. He also seized the lands and property of John of Gaunt. This was Richard's big mistake, for John of Gaunt had a son named Henry Bolingbroke. He decided to fight to regain what was his by right, and to take revenge on Richard.

Black Death and the Wars of the Roses

In Ireland, Richard's power and influence continued to weaken. By 1399 he was forced to return to Ireland to try and regain control once more. While he was here with his army, and before he could regain control, Henry Bolingbroke claimed the English throne. Richard hurried back to England, but was captured and imprisoned and died there, most probably murdered. Henry was crowned King Henry IV on 30 October 1399. But like Richard, his influence in Ireland was restricted almost entirely to the Pale, which was decreasing in size.

There are a number of reasons why the power of the English king waned in Ireland at this time. One reason is that some Norman families, like the Fitzgeralds of Kildare, had been given positions of power and influence in Ireland. Members of the Fitzgerald family served as Viceroys, but they, like many other Norman families, now regarded themselves as Irish, and resented the English in the Pale, and the power of the English king in Ireland.

Another reason why English influence in Ireland waned around this time is because English kings were fighting wars in France. You remember that the Normans came from Normandy in northern France, and from the time of William the Conqueror, English kings claimed to be kings of part of France. English armies regularly fought with the king of France to try and protect their lands there. Wars cost money and men, and this meant that the English kings could not spare money or men to fight in Ireland.

Yet another reason was that there were continual disputes in England over who was the rightful king. The most vicious and long lasting of these disputes was the Wars of the Roses. It was given this name because each side in the dispute choose a rose, just like a badge, to represent them. This war lasted thirty years and was fought between the family of the House of York, whose supporters wore a white rose, and the family of the House of Lancaster, whose supporters wore a red rose.

The House of York is in Yorkshire and one of its chief cities is Leeds. The House of Lancaster is in Lancashire and one of its chief cities is Manchester. Today, colours from that long ago War of the Roses are still worn by football teams from those two cities: Leeds United in white and

Manchester United in red. So that old rivalry still exists, but thankfully players are not killed during the matches.

But during the Wars of the Roses, it was a dangerous time to live in England, especially if you were related to, or supported, the rival claimants to the throne. When one claimant succeeded to the throne he would have all his rivals murdered, or tried for treason and beheaded. Even children were not safe, and one of the saddest stories from this time is that two young princes, Edward and Richard, were murdered while imprisoned in the Tower of London.

This murder was carried out on the orders of Richard III. He was then king, but had no right to the throne. He was of the House of York, and was a cruel man, like many of the kings from that time. He was the uncle of the princes, one of whom – Edward – was the rightful heir to the throne. Richard, like all tyrants, was frightened that when Edward grew up he would try to reclaim the throne and have Richard tried as a traitor and executed.

One night Richard sent men to the Tower of London and they murdered the two little princes while they were asleep. They buried the bodies beneath a stairway, and years afterwards they were found there. Richard denied that he was responsible for the disappearance of the princes, but the people knew that he had ordered their murder.

Because of this, and because Richard was so cruel, the people hated him. When a man named Henry Tudor decided to fight Richard for the crown, the people supported him. The armies of these two men met on 22 August 1485 at a famous place called Bosworth Field, where Richard was defeated. Though a cruel man, he was very brave, and even when the battle seemed lost, he refused to flee. He died fighting, the last reigning English king to die in battle. It is said that his crown fell off during the fighting and that when the battle was over a man named Lord Stanley found the crown on the battlefield. Lord Stanley picked it up and placed it on Henry Tudor's head while his supporters cried out, 'Long Live King Henry'. The place where Henry was crowned is still called Crown Hill today.

This Battle of Bosworth Field was the final battle in the Wars of the Roses. It ended the reign of the kings of England who were known as the Plantagenets, and which had begun with Henry II. They were called Plantagenets because an earlier member of the family, Geoffrey of Anjou, a place in France, wore a piece of broom in his cap. The Latin name for this plant is *planta genista*, from which the word Plantagenet comes.

With the death of Richard III, a new family of monarchs – the Tudors – came to reign in England. They also became the Lords of Ireland. The first of these rulers was Henry VII, who was crowned by Lord Stanley on Crown Hill.

Shortly after Henry VII became king, a young man arrived in Dublin claiming that he was the Earl of Warwick, and had a right to the English throne. He was an impostor, but the Irish people believed him and crowned him king of Ireland. He then returned to England with an army of Irish and German soldiers, intent on claiming the English crown. His army was small and ill-trained, and was defeated at the Battle of Stoke. The pretender was taken prisoner and it turned out that his name was Lambert Simnel, the son of a baker. Henry did not execute Lambert, but sent him to work in the royal kitchens. I suppose we could claim that Lambert Simnel, a baker's son, was the last king of Ireland. But, in reality, he was no such thing.

Shortly after this, another man claimed to be one of the two princes who had been murdered in the Tower of London on the orders of Richard III. But he, too, was an impostor, named Perkin Warbeck, who had been put up to this ruse by enemies of Henry's who wanted the crown for themselves. Warbeck got support from Cornwall, which is part of England, but when Henry's army came to do battle, Warbeck ran away to France. He was eventually captured and at first Henry treated him kindly. But when he found out that Warbeck was still plotting with others to overthrow him, he had the man beheaded.

Henry VII reigned as king of England and Lord of Ireland until his death in 1509. During his life, he showed little interest in Ireland. But that changed with the coronation of his son, Henry VIII. Events that took place during his reign were to have terrible consequences for the people of both England and Ireland. They led to great bloodshed and suffering yet began over the simple matter of who should be Henry's rightful wife.

14
The King with Six Wives

The disasters, which were to befall Ireland and England at the beginning of the sixteenth century, began with two weddings. The first was in 1501, when sixteen-year-old Prince Arthur, heir to the throne, married Catherine of Aragon. Two months later the young prince died. On his death, the second son of Henry VII, also named Henry, became heir to the throne. When the king died in 1509, this second son was crowned Henry VIII. He was then just eighteen years old.

Towards the end of his life, Henry VII had become greedy and cruel, and the people were glad to see an end to his reign. They hoped his son would be a better king than his father. At first, they were not disappointed. The young man was intelligent, he wrote books, music and songs, and loved wrestling and hunting. Soon his subjects came to love and admire him.

After his coronation, the second wedding took place when Henry married Catherine, his brother Arthur's widow. At this time, it was forbidden by the Catholic Church for any man to marry his brother's widow. England was a Catholic country and in order to marry Catherine, Henry had to get permission from the Pope. Unfortunately, Henry and Catherine's sons did not live. Henry blamed his wife for this, and began to worry about who should reign after his death. It was very important that a king had an heir. If he did not, then on his death there was likely to be disputes over who should be the next king. At times these disputes led to wars, something Henry wished to avoid.

Henry decided to take a new wife who, he hoped, would bear him sons. He was in love with a woman, Anne Boleyn, and wished to marry her. But in order to marry, he would have to divorce Catherine and would again need permission from the Pope to do so. This time the Pope refused permission, which angered Henry. He was a powerful king and thought that the Pope should not tell him what he could or could not do. Henry declared himself head of the Church in England, divorced Catherine and married Anne. This had little effect on Ireland, which was also a Catholic country. But later it would have terrible consequences.

Anne was a beautiful young woman and at first she and Henry were happy. Soon a daughter, Princess Elizabeth, was born, but they did not have any sons. Henry still did not have a male heir. He now decided to get rid of Anne and marry someone else. Rather than divorce Anne, he had her falsely accused of treason. When she was found guilty, she was beheaded. It was a terrible thing for Henry to do. Not only did he have his wife executed, but the little Princess Elizabeth, who was just two years old, lost her mother.

On the day after Anne's execution, Henry married Jane Seymour and they had a son, Edward. Shortly afterwards, Jane died. But despite now having an heir, Henry married three more times. He had six wives in all. You might think that he enjoyed weddings, but in fact he had become a cruel, heartless man like his father. He had two of his wives beheaded, as well as many of his best friends and advisers.

Henry, like most kings, needed a great deal of money to run his palaces and to rule the country. To raise money, he taxed the people, but still did not have enough. He was still angry with the Pope and came up with an idea of how he could have revenge on the Pope and raise the money he badly needed. He decided to close the Catholic churches, monasteries and convents in England and Ireland, and seize all their valuables and land. There were over 500 monasteries and convents in Ireland, although they were not immediately affected by Henry's decision. But over the next 100 years most were closed down or destroyed. This was a terrible blow to the people because the monasteries and convents provided education, and were also hospitals and refuges for the poor. Without their charity and medical aid, the poor suffered greatly.

There were many in England who were unhappy with Henry's actions and opposed him. Meanwhile, the Irish ignored him as his actions still did not affect them. But there were many who believed that the Catholic Church was corrupt, and they supported Henry. The people who protested against the corruption became known as Protestants, a word that originated in Germany. There, in 1517, a man named Martin Luther began to preach against the corruption in the church, which he claimed needed reforming. Luther's campaign became known as the Reformation. In 1529, German princes who supported Luther published a 'protest' against their Catholic Emperor. From this 'protest' we get the word Protestant.

This Reformation, which was sweeping Europe, affected the church in England. Henry's quarrel with the Pope, and his declaring himself head of the Church in England, helped the Reformation make the English Church Protestant. Catholics were now persecuted, and those who refused to recognise Henry as head of the Church were imprisoned or executed, and their property and lands seized.

Again, this had little effect in Ireland, except for those English settlers who lived in the Pale. Outside this area, conflicts continued between the Irish clans and those settlers who had taken their land. The king, who lived in England, could do little about this. He relied on his Viceroy, his representative in Ireland, to rule the country in his name. At this time, Gearóid Óg Fitzgerald, of the Norman family of Kildare, was the Viceroy. Gearóid Óg ruled the country to his own advantage and King Henry was so displeased with him that he had him imprisoned in the Tower of London.

Gearóid Óg had a son, who was known as Silken Thomas because he dressed in fine clothes and wore silk fringes on his jackets. When he heard a rumour, which proved to be false, that his father had been executed by Henry, he rebelled.

Henry was furious and sent an army to Ireland under the command of Sir William Skeffington. He brought artillery to Ireland for the first time and easily took the Fitzgerald castle at Maynooth. On capturing it, he had all the defenders executed. This action terrified the Irish and the Normans. It made them realise that they could not defeat such a powerful army. Fearing for their lives and their lands, many of them submitted to Henry and also recognised him as the head of the Church in Ireland.

Silken Thomas was eventually captured and taken to England with five of his uncles. All six were charged with treason and beheaded in 1537 in the Tower of London, where Gearóid Óg had already died a prisoner in 1534.

At this time, the English king still only regarded himself as Lord of Ireland. But in 1642, Henry declared himself to be the king of Ireland, thus cementing the link between the two countries. From then on, only English-born men could hold the post of Viceroy, or other important government positions. A permanent English army was also stationed in Ireland to deal with any further rebellions that might arise.

Henry declared that all Irish land belonged to the king. He then granted the land back to the owners so that they were under obligation to him, and gave them new titles. The chief of the O'Neills, who in the Gaelic tradition was known as 'The O'Neill', now became Earl of Tyrone in the English tradition. Henry rewarded those Englishmen who had supported him by granting them lands taken from the rebels. This began the policy that became known as plantation, and which later English monarchs ruthlessly pursued. It led to great hardship and turmoil for the Irish people. It signalled the beginning of the end of 2,000 years of the old Gaelic way of life, and was to be responsible for much bloodshed and slaughter in the coming centuries.

15
The Three Queens

Henry VIII died in 1547 leaving three children: Mary, Elizabeth and Edward, who was the youngest of the three. Though only nine years old, as Henry's only son, he succeeded to the throne. He was a quiet, gentle boy, who loved books, but he was also sickly and died aged fifteen in 1553. Before he died, English noblemen who wanted power for themselves forced him to make a will naming a young girl, Lady Jane Grey, as queen. She was also the queen of Ireland, but it is almost certain that the Irish didn't even know this, nor cared all that much.

Lady Jane was the great-granddaughter of Henry VII, but she was not the heir to the throne. She was Edward's cousin and had loved him dearly. At just sixteen years of age, Lady Jane was like any young girl and wanted to be having fun with her friends, and did not wish to be queen. But she was forced to agree. She reigned for just nine days before she was deposed by other noblemen who supported Henry's daughter, Mary, who was the rightful heir. Though she was the Queen of England and Ireland, poor Lady Jane Gray was arrested and imprisoned in the Tower.

Mary was a Catholic, but she was a wicked woman and immediately set about punishing Protestants. During her reign many Protestant in England were burned at the stake. When some noblemen plotted against her, she blamed the innocent Lady Jane Grey. Lady Jane, along with her husband, father and her brother were beheaded. She was then just seventeen years old and it was an evil thing for the queen to do. With all the bloodshed she was responsible for, Queen Mary earned herself the appropriate nickname 'Bloody Mary'.

She was also a stubborn woman who wanted her own way. Much against the wishes of the English people she married Philip II of Spain.

The Three Queens

Spain was a Catholic country and England's sworn enemy. At this time the Spanish were persecuting anyone they suspected of not being a true Catholic. These people were known as heretics and thousands of them were burned at the stake.

Because Mary was Catholic, the Irish people thought that she would be kind to them. But she was not. When fighting arose between the Irish clans in the counties of Offaly and Laois and the English living in the Pale, Mary's army drove out the Irish and took their land. She then gave it to English settlers, continuing the policy of plantation begun by her father and which would continue long after her death. She renamed Laois 'Queen's County' in honour of herself, and renamed Offaly 'King's County' in honour of her husband, Philip.

The dispossessed Irish families tried to win back their lands, but they were betrayed and many of them were murdered. The remaining members either fled into the woods and bogs and continued to fight, or fled westward to Kerry. In the coming years, tens of thousands of Irish people who were driven from their lands would also flee to the west of Ireland.

'Bloody Mary' died in 1558 and her half-sister, Elizabeth, became queen of England and Ireland. Elizabeth was the daughter of Anne Boleyn, and was a staunch Protestant. She had been imprisoned by 'Bloody Mary', who feared that Elizabeth might try to seize her crown.

When Elizabeth came to the throne she was determined to suppress any Irish rebellion that might break out and intended to continue the policy of plantation. The Irish who rebelled would have their lands taken and given to loyal Protestant English and Scottish settlers. The Viceroys, who had been Englishmen since the time of 'Silken Thomas', enforced English laws in Ireland with extreme brutality. This brutality even extended to the Norman families. They were also Catholics, and were seen as enemies of the queen, who was now head of the Protestant Church in England and Ireland.

Most of the Irish clans were frightened of rebelling, aware that if they did so their lands would be seized. But one man, Shane O'Neill, did rebel. His father was the Earl of Tyrone and following his death Shane became head of the clan. But he refused to accept the title of Earl, and still called himself 'The O'Neill' in the old tradition. He proclaimed that Ulster belonged to his family and that he would make it his. Because of his boasts, he was known as 'Shane the Proud'.

In 1562 he rebelled and attacked the MacDonnells of Antrim, who were old enemies, and defeated them at Glenshesk. The English tried to poison him and when that failed, they persuaded the O'Donnells of Donegal to attack him. The two armies met near Letterkenny and in the ensuing battle Shane was defeated. Foolishly, he fled to the MacDonnells seeking their help. Though they pretended to welcome him, they were still bitter at their defeat at Glenshesk and murdered Shane. They pickled his head to preserve it and sent it to Dublin Castle where it was stuck on a spike at the entrance, a dire warning to anyone else who might be considering rebellion.

Despite this grim warning, a rebellion broke out in Munster. Some of the finest land in Ireland was in the province, and many Englishmen wished to possess it. One of the most important families in Munster was the Fitzgeralds. They were Normans and known as the Geraldines. They bitterly resented the English queen being head of the Irish Church, and were also angered by English interference in Munster, which was intended to make them rebel. At first they resisted rebellion, fearful of losing their land. But eventually they were forced to rebel.

The rebellion was just what the English had been waiting for. They invaded Munster and laid waste to the province. There was fearful slaughter, both of people and animals. It has been claimed that from Limerick to Kerry not a single cow could be heard lowing. Those people who survived the slaughter fled into the bogs and woods where most died of starvation and disease.

The Irish sought help from Spain, which was England's enemy. A small Spanish force of about 800 landed at Smerwick, near Dingle in County Kerry. The English soldiers surrounded them in the fort of Dún an Óir and, outnumbered, the Spanish surrendered. They were shown no mercy and all of them were brutally slaughtered. When the rebellion was over, the best land in Munster was confiscated and given to English settlers, a policy which would be pursued with utter ruthlessness in the years to come. Among those who were given land were the seafarer Sir Walter Raleigh, and the poet Edmund Spenser, who wrote *The Faerie Queen*.

The Irish still hoped that help might come from Spain, which was still a strong Catholic country. You remember that Philip II, king of Spain had married 'Bloody Mary'. After her death, he wished to marry Elizabeth, but she refused him. Bitterly angry at this, and because England was one of Spain's greatest enemies, he decided to invade the country. In 1588 a great Spanish force of about 130 warships, known as the Spanish Armada, set out from Spain bound for England. The English, who had always hated and feared the Spanish, and who now hated them even more because they were still Catholics, were ready and waiting. The Irish, however, wanted a Spanish victory, hoping that the Catholic King Philip II would look kindly on Ireland.

One of the greatest English seamen of that time was Sir Francis Drake. In 1587 he had attacked the Spanish fleet at Cadiz and burned around forty ships. He said afterwards that he had 'singed the king of Spain's beard'. Drake was playing bowls when the Spanish fleet was sighted off the English coast. The huge armada of around 130 ships would surely have terrified most men, but Drake was a brave man. He finished his game of bowls before he and his navy sailed out to meet the enemy.

A great battle raged for almost a week. Hugh cannons boomed and the air was thick with smoke and the noise of battle and the screams and shouts of the sailors. The English ships, though smaller, were an equal match for the enemy's larger, gilded vessels. English ships, known as 'hellburners', sailed in among the Spanish vessels. These 'hellburners' were first filled with gunpowder and then set on fire. In those times ships were built of timber and the 'hellburners' set fire to many enemy vessels.

Before the outcome of the battle was decided, a great storm blew up. The English took shelter along their coastline. The Spanish, however, could not use the English coast for shelter, and were helplessly driven along by the storm. Many ships were wrecked on the rocks while others foundered. Some ships were driven all the way to Ireland and wrecked along the west coast. With the loss of the Armada, Ireland now seemed without hope.

The only part which had not been completely subdued was Ulster, and there was a man there who still believed that he could defeat the English. He was Hugh O'Neill, and he had succeeded Shane O'Neill as head of the O'Neills of Tyrone. Hugh was educated in England and had attended Elizabeth's court. She was very fond of him, and had appointed him Earl of Tyrone in 1585. But despite this, O'Neill saw himself as a proud Irishman. His family had once been the most powerful family in Ireland. He felt that his land and title were his by right, and not a right to be granted him by an English queen.

In 1590, Hugh Roe MacMahon, Lord of Monaghan, raided the lands of an English settler, the Earl of Essex. An English army marched against Hugh Roe, who was captured and hanged. His lands were then confiscated and divided up between local families loyal to the English. The lands of both east and west Breifne were also confiscated and given to loyal families. After this, the English tried to seize the lands of the Maguires of Fermanagh, who rose in rebellion.

This alarmed Hugh O'Neill. He suspected that eventually the English would try to seize his lands too. He decided to join the rebellion of the Maguires and drive the English out of Ulster. He persuaded the O'Donnells of Donegal to help him and in August 1594 he attacked an English force bringing food and munitions to Enniskillen. The English soldiers were routed and they left so much food behind that the site of the battle became known as 'The Ford of the Biscuits'. This battle was to be the first in a war that is known as 'the Nine Years' War'. It began with great success but led to one of the saddest events in Irish history – the Flight of the Earls.

16
The Flight of the Earls

O'Neill's greatest ally in the Nine Years' War was Red Hugh O'Donnell. As a youth, Red Hugh had been lured into a trap by the English who imprisoned him in Dublin Castle. Now, if the O'Donnells rebelled, Red Hugh would be killed. Locked up in a prison cell and missing the hills of his beloved Donegal, he dreamed of escape. He did escape in 1591, but was betrayed and recaptured. Returned to prison, he languished in a dungeon for another year.

Then, on Christmas night 1592, he and two companions made a daring escape through a sewer. It was snowing and bitterly cold, but the three made their way to Wicklow. Here, Hugh's companions fell down exhausted and he went to get help. When he returned, his companions had died of cold and exhaustion. Hugh made his way home to Donegal and the following year, at twenty years of age, he became chief of the O'Donnells. After his imprisonment, he had good reason to dislike the English, and was ready to join Hugh O'Neill in rebellion.

The rebellion began successfully in 1595 when the rebels captured Blackwater Fort in County Armagh and won another battle at Clontibret in County Monaghan. O'Neill knew he couldn't defeat the English without help, and asked Philip III, who was now king of Spain, for soldiers. Spain was still at war with England, and Philip sent two Armadas to Ireland, but both were wrecked by fierce storms, leaving the rebels to fight on alone.

In 1598, Sir Henry Bagenal, the English commander, marched north with a large force, intent on crushing the rebellion. O'Neill and O'Donnell laid a trap for him. They dug a ditch in boggy ground at a place called the Yellow Ford, and lured Bagenal's forces there. When a cannon got stuck in the bog, Bagenal tried to pull it out. During the attempt he was shot dead and this demoralised his forces. The Irish routed the English in one of the greatest victories ever by the Irish over their enemy.

This victory, and others which followed, alarmed Queen Elizabeth. She sent her favourite Englishman, the Earl of Essex, to Ireland with 20,000 men. But he was no great leader and tried to make peace. Elizabeth summoned him back to England and, after being accused of plotting against her, he was beheaded. Elizabeth next sent Lord Mountjoy to Ireland to subdue the rebels. He was utterly ruthless and ravaged the country, slaughtering and burning and terrorising the people so that those who were not killed died of starvation and disease.

O'Neill again asked the Spanish for help and another Armada with 6,000 men set out for Ireland. Once more storms intervened and about 4,000 eventually reached Ireland. Instead of landing in the north, where the rebels were strongest, the Spaniards landed at Kinsale, County Cork, in October 1601.

Lord Mountjoy marched to Kinsale and surrounded the Spaniards. Meanwhile, O'Neill and O'Donnell set out to march nearly 500 kilometres south to support the Spanish. It was wintertime and bitterly cold, and much of the country had already been ravaged by Mountjoy. There was little food or shelter to be had, and the rebels could only struggle on day after day.

Just before Christmas 1601, they reached Kinsale and surrounded Mountjoy and his forces, trapping him between themselves and the Spanish. They could now have waited until Mountjoy ran out of food and was forced to surrender. Had this happened, it would have been a great victory for the Irish, and could have ended English rule in the country.

But instead of waiting, the Irish attacked. It was a disastrous decision. The ground was not suited to the way the Irish fought, but was perfectly suited to a well-trained English army. The Irish were still recovering from their long march and, to make matters worse, their plans were betrayed to Mountjoy by an informer. Signals to the Spanish to attack were never given, or were misunderstood. The night was dark and wet and this caused more confusion.

When the Irish attacked on Christmas Eve 1601, Lord Mountjoy was well prepared. A fierce, bloody battle raged in which the Irish were routed. O'Neill retreated north with the remnants of his army while O'Donnell managed to escape with the Spanish who had survived. He then travelled to Spain seeking further help. The English sent a spy named Blake to Spain to kill O'Donnell. Blake succeeded in poisoning O'Donnell's food and the great Red Hugh died in September 1602. He was then only twenty-nine years old.

Also in 1602 the English attacked the castle of O'Sullivan Beare, chieftain of the O'Sullivans of Beara and Bantry in west Cork. They destroyed his castle and took his land. With no land and no home, he with his family and followers set out to march hundreds of kilometres to the home of their relatives, the O'Rourkes of Breifne. The winter was still bitterly cold with heavy snow, and the marchers had little food and hardly any shelter. Everywhere they went they were attacked by both English and Irish enemies and many of them were killed. Others died of hunger and cold and disease. At one point they had to cross the Shannon, but there was no bridge, and they had no boats. They killed some of their horses, kept the flesh for food, and used the skins, along with branches cut from trees, to build makeshift boats. With these they eventually crossed the river and continued their march.

After marching for over two weeks they reached O'Rourke's castle, where they were warmly welcomed. About 1,000 men, women and children set out on the march, but only thirty-four survived to enter the castle, though a few stragglers did arrive in the following days.

With the rebellion at an end, the English soldiers again ravaged parts of the country, leaving it unfit for humans or animals to live there. It was a policy that the English forces would employ numerous times in their coming wars against the Irish, a policy by which it was intended to rule Ireland by terror and brute force if necessary.

Hugh O'Neill reached Ulster but his days were numbered, and he surrendered in 1603. Surprisingly, he was not executed, but was allowed to return to his home in Tyrone. However, he did not feel safe there, not even when Elizabeth died in 1603. So great was O'Neill's fear for his life, and that of his family, that he decided to flee Ireland. The O'Donnells, Maguires and other Ulster families joined him.

These old Gaelic families, whose origins stretched back some 2,000 years, men women and children, sailed from Rathmullen, County Donegal, on 4 September 1607, an event known as the 'Flight of the Earls'. Many of them stood on deck as the ship, with sails billowing in the wind, put out to sea. There was much crying among the women and children as they realised they were leaving their homes and their homeland forever. The men's faces seemed carved from stone, but inside they, too, felt desolate. They had fought long and bravely, but eventually had been defeated by a stronger and more ruthless foe.

Hugh O'Neill never saw Ireland again. He died in Rome in 1616 far from his beloved land, the last of the great Irish chieftains. The other families were scattered throughout Europe, many of the men joining the armies of France and Spain where they excelled themselves. Today, the names of some of those Gaelic families can still be found in European countries.

That date – 4 September 1607 – is one of the saddest in Irish history. It signalled the beginning of the end of the old Gaelic Ireland, which had existed from the time of the Celts some 2,000 years before. This old Gaelic Ireland had experienced the coming of Christianity, the Golden Age of peace and learning, the invasion and eventual defeat of the Vikings and the arrival of the Normans, who became as Irish as the old Gaelic families themselves. Now the Gaelic people who remained in Ireland were to become strangers in their own country, and were to suffer even greater hardships than those who had gone before them.

The English were now determined that the Irish should never again rebel and resorted to ruthless plantation as a means of achieving this. They confiscated the lands of the earls who had fled and gave them to English and Scottish settlers. Part of what was County Derry was given to a company from London, and they renamed the area Londonderry. These new settlers were Protestants, and the Catholic Irish who still

The Flight of the Earls

remained in Ulster now found themselves as tenants or labourers on their own land. The Protestant settlers did not treat their Catholic tenants or labourers very well, and this led to much resentment.

Though the English succeeded in taking much of the Irish land, their other objective, which was to enforce the Protestant religion on the Irish people, failed: they remained Catholic. Land and power and religion now divided the people who lived in Ireland. On one side were the Irish and Norman Catholic people who had been dispossessed, and on the other side the English and Scottish Protestant settlers who had taken their land. This situation bred bitterness and a desire for revenge, and led to one of the most brutal of all Irish rebellions. Before it took place there was a bloody war in England. Like the Wars of the Roses, it was fought over the question of who should rule. However, it wasn't fought between rival kings, but between King Charles II and the English Parliament. Charles lost and was beheaded. The man who defeated him was Oliver Cromwell, and he was destined to become the most feared and hated Englishman ever to bring an army to Ireland. What occurred while he was here with his army is still known as 'the curse of Cromwell'.

17
The Curse of Cromwell

Before I tell you about 'the curse of Cromwell', we must return to the history of England. When Queen Elizabeth I died in 1603, she left no heir to the throne. She was the last of the Tudors, a monarchy that began, you remember, with Henry VII, the victor in the War of the Roses. The next in line to succeed Elizabeth was James Stuart, who was then king of Scotland. He was a nephew of Henry VIII, and Elizabeth's nearest relative.

James was crowned James I in 1603, the first of the Stuart kings of England, Ireland, Scotland and Wales. Now, for the very first time, the English king could claim to rule all four countries. Since the time of Edward I, English monarchs had wanted to rule Scotland. Ironically, under a Scottish king, this had come to pass.

James was a Protestant, and did not treat his Catholic subjects very well. This angered them, and some of them plotted to kill him. The date set for carrying out this plot was 5 November 1603 when the king attended the official opening of parliament in London.

The leader of the plotters was Guy Fawkes. He and his supporters hid barrels of gunpowder in the cellars beneath the Houses of Parliament. Their plan was to blow up the building, killing the king and his followers. However, the king learned of this plot and Guy Fawkes was arrested on 4 November along with most of his supporters. All of them were later executed.

The Curse of Cromwell

Did you know that the failure of Guy Fawkes to blow up parliament is still celebrated in England with bonfires and fireworks on the 5 November? At almost all the bonfires they also burn an effigy, which is called 'The Guy'. This effigy is actually an effigy of Guy Fawkes, which is why it's burned and why it's called 'The Guy'.

James I ruled until his death in 1625. He had wanted to have all the power for himself and dismissed parliament for a number of years. During his reign, English and Scottish settlers continued to arrive in Ireland to take over land, or to rent land from English landlords. With the departure of the great chieftains of Ulster, there were few left in Ireland to offer opposition, and any hint of rebellion was ruthlessly put down. The Irish people continued to suffer greatly from hunger and disease, but no major rebellions broke out. War, however, broke out in England.

There were two main reasons for this war. The first had its origins in religion. During the reign of James I, many Protestants thought that the Church of England should be plain and without ornament. They also didn't want to use the official prayer book, the Book of Common Prayer, in their services. Many of these Protestants also believed that it was a sin to wear brightly coloured clothes, or have any fun. Because of this attitude, they were called Puritans.

They were persecuted for their beliefs and about 100 of them fled England and went to America on a famous ship, the *Mayflower*. They are known as the Pilgrim Fathers, and they called the place where they landed in America, Plymouth, which was the port in England from which they sailed. The area where they settled they called New England. However, many Puritans still remained in England. They hated the king and his supporters because they seemed to spend their time hunting and feasting and drinking.

When the much-disliked James I died, his son, Charles, became King Charles I. He was much like his father and he, too, quarrelled with parliament. He also tried to force the Scots to use the Book of Common Prayer in their churches. But the Scottish Protestants were proud of their own religion, which was known as Presbyterianism. They held views similar to those of the Puritans. They rebelled against Charles and a Scottish army marched into England. The English Puritans supported them and Charles was forced to allow the Scots to practise their own type of Protestantism.

Unfortunately, Charles didn't learn a lesson from this and continued to quarrel with parliament. This quarrel got so bad that civil war broke out. On one side were the king and his supporters, who were known as Royalists. They were also known as Cavaliers, a word which is derived from the Spanish word for a horseman, because most of them rode horses. They wore their hair long and curled, and wore flamboyant clothes and believed in enjoying themselves.

On the other side was the parliament, which represented the common people. These were known as Parliamentarians, or Roundheads. This latter name was given to them because their hair was cut short, and it looked like an upturned bowl on their heads. Many were Puritans, and they hated the king and his Cavaliers, and were determined to defeat them. They were not as well trained or as well armed as the Cavaliers, but they had a strong, brilliant leader, Oliver Cromwell. Under him, they became so powerful and successful in battle that they were known as Ironsides. They utterly defeated the king's forces in a great battle at Naseby, Northamptonshire, on 14 June 1645. Charles fled to Scotland, but was captured and brought back to London. He was tried for high treason and executed in January 1649, and for the next eleven years there was no king.

While the civil war was being fought in England, a rebellion broke out in Ireland. In 1641, the anger and resentment, which had been festering against the new settlers, erupted. The Irish Catholic people, aware of the civil war in England, saw it as an opportunity to rebel against those who had taken their lands. The date set for the rebellion was October 1641.

The rebellion was badly planned and an attack on Dublin Castle, the base of English power in Ireland, never took place. Rebellion did break out in Ulster, led by Phelim O'Neill, and many terrible atrocities were committed against the Protestant settlers. The worst atrocity occurred in

November 1641 when 100 men, women and children were murdered on a bridge at Portadown, many being thrown into the River Bann and drowned. Atrocities were also committed by Protestants against Catholics, and the rebellion was both cruel and bloody. It struck fresh terror in the Protestant people, and made them even more fearful. This fear was so strong that it never eased, and it still exists in the north of Ireland to this very day.

The rebels soon held most of Ulster and marched south to attack Drogheda and Dundalk. They were joined by Norman families who had lost their lands, and who were also suffering religious persecution. The leaders, Irish and Norman, along with other important men, met in Kilkenny in October 1642 to discuss what should happen next. This meeting, which is known as the Confederation of Kilkenny, was virtually an Irish parliament. Unfortunately, distrust arose between the Irish and the Norman members and the Confederation failed.

The English appealed to the Scots for help and a Scottish army under General Munro landed at Carrickfergus, County Antrim, in April 1642. Munro marched south to engage the rebels in Leinster, who were still commanded by Phelim O'Neill. He was a poor leader and the rebels were feeling demoralised when Owen Roe O'Neill, a nephew of the great Hugh O'Neill, returned to Ireland from the continent and took over the leadership. He had served in the Spanish army and was a brilliant soldier.

When O'Neill learned of Munro's march south he realised that he would have to stop him joining with the rest of the English army. O'Neill led his men to a place called Benburb, County Tyrone, determined to prevent Munro going any further. On 4 May 1646, the two armies met in a fierce battle. Munro and his soldiers suffered a terrible defeat and retreated in disarray.

O'Neill now decided to march on Dublin and join up with another group of rebels led by a man named Preston. But Preston betrayed O'Neill, who returned to Ulster with his soldiers. Preston's army was eventually defeated on Dangan Hill, County Meath, while another group of rebels was defeated at Knocknanoss, near Mallow, County Cork. O'Neill's army was still undefeated, but the rebellion was already lost, and the Catholic people of Ireland were about to pay an unimaginable price for it.

The rebellion infuriated Oliver Cromwell, who was now the most powerful man in England. When he learned of the atrocities against the Protestants, he swore to punish those who had committed them. He was determined to enforce English rule in Ireland and ensure that there never again would be a rebellion, nor would Protestants be massacred. He was also intent on making Ireland a Protestant, Puritan country.

Like all tyrants, blinded by his own twisted beliefs, he refused to believe that massacres and atrocities had also been carried out by Protestants, and by English and Scottish soldiers. Nor did he wish to acknowledge the injustices that had been done to the Irish people. Instead, he chose to believe the lie that tens of thousands of Protestants had been murdered, and was intent on avenging their deaths.

With an army of 20,000 men, Cromwell landed in Dublin on 15 August 1649, one of the darkest days in all Ireland's long history. He was intent on revenge, and crushing all opposition to his rule. The headquarters of those who opposed him was in Drogheda. The soldiers there were not Irish, nor did they have an Irish leader. They were English soldiers who had supported King Charles, and were led by an English Catholic, Sir Arthur Ashton.

Drogheda was a fortified town, but the thick walls were quickly breached by Cromwell's artillery, and the town was taken on 11 September 1649. Cromwell, a cruel, merciless man, driven by religious fanaticism, ordered that all the soldiers in the town should be put to death. However, his bloodthirsty soldiers showed no mercy to anyone, and ordinary men, women and children were also massacred. Sir William Ashton was beaten to death with his own wooden leg. The soldiers thought that the hollow leg contained gold but it did not.

Townspeople, terrified by the awful slaughter, sought refuge in Saint Peter's Church. There were a great many women and children among them, as well as the elderly and the sick. They huddled together in the church amidst much wailing and crying, hoping that they would be spared. But the soldiers were driven wild with bloodlust. They set fire to the church, and those within who were not burned to death were massacred as they tried to escape.

With Drogheda secure, Cromwell marched south. Terrorstricken by what had happened at Drogheda, other towns surrendered. Some of the people in these towns were treated fairly well. But Wexford suffered a similar fate to Drogheda. The town had agreed to surrender, but before that happened, Cromwell attacked. Here again, the defenders as well as the innocent inhabitants were massacred.

Cromwell continued his course of revenge against the Irish people by taking their land. He then planted it with his supporters and soldiers as a reward for their loyalty. He gave the Irish a simple choice. They could flee 'to hell or to Connacht'. Those who could flee to Connacht did so, and the countryside was thronged with thousands of terrified men, women and children fleeing for their lives. Connacht had the poorest land in Ireland and many of those who fled there found no sanctuary, but died of hunger and disease. Those who survived were the lucky ones, if one could call those who'd lost everything, and had to flee for their lives, lucky.

Those who could not flee quickly died of hunger and disease, or were hunted down by Cromwell's soldiers and killed. During those years, tens of thousands of Irish men, women and children perished in war, or died from starvation and disease. Such was the calamity to befall Ireland that it became known as the 'curse of Cromwell'. It ensured that he would be the most feared and hated man Ireland had ever known, or would ever know.

Cromwell returned to England in 1650 and declared himself Lord Protector of the people and ruled with an iron fist. Though hated by Catholics, and those who had supported the king, nevertheless he was greatly admired by his own Protestant people, and by the Protestant people of Europe. They saw him not as a tyrant but as the guardian of their rights and their Protestant faith.

Oliver Cromwell died on 3 September 1658 and his son, Richard, became Lord Protector. But he soon gave up the position and in 1660 the son of Charles I returned from exile and was crowned Charles II. He was secretly a Roman Catholic, though he pretended to be a Protestant. He persecuted those who had been involved in the trial and execution of his father, and had many of them executed. He also banished many Protestants, who went to live in Holland, which was a Protestant country. Thirty years later, a Dutch Protestant, William of Orange, would become king of England and Ireland. This event was to lead to another battle fought on Irish soil. This battle, one of the last great battles fought in Ireland, took place on 12 July 1690, and is known as The Battle of the Boyne.

18
The Battle of the Boyne

The Battle of the Boyne was fought between a Catholic king and a Protestant king, both of whom claimed the right to the English throne. This situation arose because when Charles II died in 1685, he left no heir. On his death, his brother James was crowned King James II. He was a Catholic, and wished to restore the Catholic religion to his kingdom. Like many other kings, he was a cruel man, and his supporters carried out terrible atrocities against Protestants, especially in Scotland. The people's hatred of James grew and, when a son was born, they realised that he would succeed his father. They would continue to have a Catholic monarchy, something they wished to avoid, and they acted to prevent this.

James's daughter, Mary, was married to Prince William of the Dutch House of Orange. Both were Protestants and the English people asked them to be their king and queen. They accepted, and on 5 November 1688, William landed with his army at Torbay in southern England. He was a small man but, riding on a great white horse, and with his polished armour gleaming, he looked every inch a king as rode into London. There, he and his wife were crowned king and queen.

When James learned that William was on his way to England, he fled to France with his wife and son. There he asked Louis XIV for help. Louis was at war with the Dutch and offered to help James. He gave him soldiers and with these James sailed for Ireland. He knew the Irish would not support William, the Protestant king, but would support James because he was a Catholic. Like Edward Bruce before him, James saw an opportunity to win back his throne by fighting a war in Ireland.

James landed at Kinsale in March 1689 and marched to Dublin. The country was still devastated by the previous wars and the displacement of the Irish population. Hunger and disease were rife and the Protestant settlers were living in a state of fear. There was famine too, and food was difficult to obtain. When the Protestant settlers in Ulster learned of James's arrival, they left their lands and sought refuge in the towns of Enniskillen and Derry.

James's forces now marched on Derry. The city was fortified with walls, yet as the army approached the people in the town grew terrified. They feared that if they resisted the attackers, they would be massacred if the town was taken. They decided to surrender, but a group of thirteen young Protestant apprentices, who happened to be in the city, raced to the gates and closed them. The attackers had no other choice but to lay siege to the city. They surrounded the walls and built a wooden barrier across the River Foyle, on which Derry was built. This barrier, or boom, was designed to prevent ships sailing up the river with food and water to relieve the city.

The siege lasted 105 days. During this time no food was allowed into the city. As a result of this, the people inside the walls were soon starving. Yet they would not yield, even when, having eaten all the horses and dogs, the people were forced to eat rats and mice, and even to chew the skins of the animals. Disease soon spread and about 4,000 people – half the population of the city – died.

Their only hope was that help would come from England. But no help came. When the soldiers and the people were barely able to stand, never mind fight, and were on the verge of surrendering, three ships were glimpsed sailing up the Foyle. The longed-for help had come at last.

The leading ship was the *Mountjoy*, and she sailed straight at the boom. Those besieging the city, and those within, held their breaths as the ship smashed into the barrier. There was a tremendous crashing sound, but the boom, though damaged, held firm. The *Mountjoy* was damaged and sank into the mud of the river. The besiegers cheered while those within the walls groaned in despair. It seemed as if they were doomed.

The second of the three ships now sailed directly toward the boom. Again there was a tremendous crashing noise. The already-damaged boom broke apart and the ship passed through and sailed on into the city. It was the inhabitants' turn to cheer while the besiegers looked on in dismay, knowing that the siege had failed. They had no other choice but to withdraw. The war, however, was not yet over.

William decided to come to Ireland and engage James in battle. William arrived in Carrickfergus in the summer of 1690, and was joined by other soldiers in Ulster. At the head of 40,000 men, he marched south towards Dublin, while James, with 26,000 men, marched north.

The two armies met at the River Boyne on 12 July 1690. The scene of the battle is not far from Drogheda, where Oliver Cromwell had carried out his first massacre forty-one years before. William's army was well armed and well trained, while James's soldiers were poorly armed and poorly disciplined. William was a fine leader while James was almost useless, and was also a cowardly man.

The outcome of the battle was inevitable. James's army was defeated and he fled the battlefield. It is said that when he reached Dublin he told a woman there that he had lost the battle because his 'cowardly Irish troops had run away'. The woman, no doubt aware of James's cowardly reputation, replied: 'Then it seems Your Majesty has won the race'. James continued his flight and returned to France, leaving his Irish supporters to fight on in his name. The Protestant people of Ulster celebrated King William's victory at the Boyne, and still do so every year on 12 July when they march through the cities and towns of Northern Ireland.

After his victory at the Boyne, William took Dublin. Meanwhile, the Irish and French soldiers retreated west, intending to halt William's advance across the River Shannon at Limerick and Athlone. In Limerick, one of the Irish commanders was Patrick Sarsfield. He was a brave man, who had fought in the French army, and he was determined that Limerick would not surrender.

William's army marched west to lay siege to Limerick in August 1690. The city was defended by strong walls, and heavy artillery would be needed to breach them. Over 150 wagons laden with cannon, cannonballs and barrels of gunpowder, and drawn by hundreds of horses, set out from Dublin, bound for the attackers.

Sarsfield learned of this wagon train and realised that if William's army got the artillery they would be able to breach the walls. The Irish had no choice but to prevent the wagon train from reaching the attackers. At midnight on 11 August, Sarsfield, along with a troop of cavalry, slipped out of the city under the cover of darkness. Their plan was to find the wagon train and blow it up.

The wagon train had stopped overnight at Ballyneety, nor far from Limerick city. But Sarsfield and his men could not ride directly there because William's army was between them and Ballyneety. They had to take a roundabout route through the dark countryside. Sarsfield was not familiar with the area, and he and his men were guided by a man named 'Galloping' Michael Hogan. He was a raparee, a type of highwayman, and was so nicknamed because he usually rode a horse. Stories claim that earlier that day Hogan had stopped to buy apples from an old woman, and she had told him that the password to be used that night by those guarding the wagon train was none other than 'Sarsfield'.

'Galloping' Hogan led Sarsfield and his men through the dark countryside to Ballyneety. When challenged for the password by soldiers guarding the wagon train, Sarsfield shouted out: 'Sarsfield is the word and Sarsfield is the man'. The soldiers, caught off guard, were quickly overpowered. The cannon, cannonballs and barrels of gunpowder were piled up in a gigantic heap. A fuse was laid and lit by Hogan.

The glare from the massive explosion momentarily turned the night into day. The deafening boom resounded about the countryside and was heard by both the attackers and the defenders. Within the walls, the people cheered, aware that Sarsfield and his men had been successful. However, their good cheer was not to last long as William's men obtained more artillery from Waterford and the siege began.

The attackers bombarded the walls for weeks, and eventually breached them in places. An attack was ordered, and fierce fighting ensued. The women of Limerick fought alongside their men, pouring boiling water down on the attackers who were eventually driven back with huge losses. William was forced to give up the siege and he returned to England, leaving a Dutchman, General Ginkell, in charge.

The Battle of the Boyne

By now, Ireland east of the Shannon was under the control of William's army. Without help from France, it was only a matter of time before Ginkell would also control the country west of the Shannon. Help did eventually come from France in May 1691 when a French general, St Ruth, arrived in Ireland. He decided to try and hold Athlone against Ginkell's forces.

On 23 June 1691, Ginkell's artillery began to pound Athlone. It was the heaviest artillery bombardment ever seen in Ireland. After days of bombardment, the bridge across the Shannon was damaged. Ginkell's troops repaired it with planks and got ready to cross it and take the town. It seemed as if nothing could stop them.

In one of the most courageous episodes in Irish history, a man named Costume asked for volunteers to help him dislodge the planks. Nine men volunteered and, led by Costume, dashed onto the bridge under fierce fire from the besiegers. The ten men succeeded in tearing up some of the planks before all of then were killed in a hail of shot. More volunteers were called for and another ten men rushed onto the bridge. They succeeded in tearing up the remaining planks, but not before eight of them died in the intense fire. Two escaped by jumping into the river and swimming to safety. St Ruth, who was a brave soldier, and who had seen many brave men in battle, claimed that it was the bravest action he had ever seen.

The bravery of the twenty men saved Athlone for the moment. Eventually, the besiegers crossed the river at another point, and took the town on 30 June 1691. St Ruth decided to retreat and fight one last battle against Ginkell's forces. This battle was fought at Aughrim, near Ballinasloe in County Galway, on 22 July 1691. Though greatly outnumbered, the Irish fought with the same courage shown by the twenty men who tore up the bridge at Athlone. The Irish might have won, except that tragedy struck. During the battle, St Ruth was killed by a cannonball and, on seeing this, the Irish soldiers lost heart. Ginkell pressed on to victory and the Irish were routed. It is claimed that more Irishmen died in the Battle of Aughrim than in any other battle ever fought in Ireland.

After his victory at Aughrim, Ginkell took the city of Galway. Only Limerick still held out and, under the command of Patrick Sarsfield, the city prepared again for a siege. Once more, Ginkell's forces surrounded the walls, but still could not take the city. It was stalemate, and eventually both sides agreed on a treaty. This treaty, known as the Treaty of Limerick, was signed on the Treaty Stone on 3 October 1691. It granted Catholics the right to practise their religion, along with many other rights. Sarsfield and his soldiers agreed to leave Ireland and go to France or Spain, where they could join the armies there.

Sarsfield, and up to 20,000 Irish soldiers, did go to fight in the armies of France and Spain. Because of their flight from the country, they are known as The Wild Geese. Like the Flight of the Earls nearly 100 years earlier, it was a tragedy for Ireland and its people. Once again, those who might have fought to defend the people sailed away from the country. Once more, Ireland and its people were left helpless and undefended. Sarsfield, and those who left, later distinguished themselves in battle. Sarsfield himself was killed fighting for the French at the Battle of Landan in 1693.

He had left Ireland believing that he had gained freedom and rights for his people. But he had hardly left when the Treaty of Limerick was broken. It is said that it was broken 'before the ink with which it was writ was dry'. With the breaking of the treaty, Ireland now entered one of the darkest periods in all of her history. In the coming centuries the old Gaelic, Catholic Ireland was utterly destroyed and replaced by a Protestant-dominated Ireland. The Irish parliament, made up of Protestant English and Scottish settlers was determined that the Irish Catholic population would never again threaten their power. Now they passed laws, known as the Penal Laws, which were the most anti-Irish, and anti-Catholic laws ever enacted in Ireland. They ensured that for almost 150 years the Protestants would have complete domination in Ireland, a period that is known as the Protestant Ascendancy.

19
Ireland's Darkest Time

At the beginning of the eighteenth century, the Irish Catholic population was demoralised. By now, Catholics owned only 15 per cent of all the land in Ireland and this caused great hardship as they struggled to survive. But worse was to come when the Protestant parliament passed the Penal Laws. More severe than the Statutes of Kilkenny, they were the harshest laws ever enacted against the native population. There were a great number of these Penal Laws, but the most important were:

Catholics could not buy land.
Catholics could not be educated.
Catholics were restricted in practising their religion.
Catholics could not sit in parliament, or even vote in an election.
Catholics could not become barristers, judges, or sit on a jury.
Catholics could not hold public office.
Catholics could not live in certain towns.
A Catholic could not own a horse worth more than £5.
A Catholic could not carry arms, or join the English army.

Under the severity of these laws, Protestant control of the country became almost complete. But though unable to fight for their freedom, the Irish did not give in. They founded hedge schools where children were taught by travelling teachers, usually in the open air, using a hedge for shelter. Priests, who were hunted like wild animals and murdered if they were caught, said Mass in the open, using a flat rock for an altar. Today, Mass rocks can still be seen dotted about the Irish countryside.

Yet the Irish Catholics remained a subdued population in their own country. English landlords charged high rents, and when a tenant farmer was unable to pay, he and his family were evicted. It was at this time that some Irish Catholics emigrated, a trend that would increase to a veritable flood in the next century, when hundreds of thousands fled the Great Famine of 1845–1847.

Some Catholics founded secret societies and attacked landlords and their agents. The best known of these societies were the Defenders and the Whiteboys. The latter were so named because its members wore white shirts, or smocks, when they went out at night to destroy crops, or maim cattle, or attack people. This society was most active in Munster, and was led by men with fictitious names like Captain Moonlight. The Defenders were most active in Ulster, and here the Protestants formed their own societies to counteract them. The best known of these Protestant societies was the Peep o' Day Boys.

There was much conflict between these two groups and both were responsible for terrible atrocities. On 21 September 1795, the two groups fought each other near Loughgall, County Armagh, at a place known as The Diamond. It was a small fight, but its aftermath led to a significant moment in Irish history. After the fight, the Peep o' Day Boys entered Loughgall where James Sloan, Daniel Winter and James Wilson founded the Orange Order. It was to be one of the most important Protestant societies ever founded in Ireland. It encouraged hatred of Catholics and this led to much strife, bloodshed and death in the years to come.

But not all Protestants hated Catholics. A Protestant, Henry Grattan, believed that Irish Catholics were treated harshly and wanted to repeal the Penal Laws. He was partially successful and some Penal Laws, relating to land ownership and inheritance rights, were repealed. Yet Catholics still suffered greatly and seemed without hope until two events, which occurred outside Ireland, gave them fresh optimism. The first was the American War of Independence in which the American people won their independence from Britain. Some Irishmen began to believe that if the Americans could win independence, then the Irish people could do so too.

Ireland's Darkest Time

The second event was a much more important one than the American War of Independence. This was the French Revolution of 1789. At this time, France was ruled by a king, Louis XVI, and his wife, Marie Antoinette. The royal family lived in great luxury in their many palaces. One of these palaces at Versailles, outside Paris, was one of the most magnificent palaces in the whole world.

The French nobles owned large estates, and they, too, lived in magnificent palaces. They were able to do this because they exploited the ordinary French people, who were forced to work for little money and lived in abject poverty. The king needed vast sums of money to pay for all his fine palaces, and his life of luxury, and so was constantly in debt. To obtain more money, he raised taxes until the people could no longer pay. They were so poor that they could not even afford to buy bread, and the poorer families were starving. Marie Antoinette, on being told of this, asked why they didn't eat cake, which was a luxury then. She was so sheltered in her palaces that she wasn't aware of the suffering of the ordinary people, and did not know that they couldn't afford to buy bread.

This suffering led to great unrest among the population and the angry people of Paris stormed the Bastille prison on 14 July 1789. It was the first action in a revolution that sought to gain for the people of France liberty, equality and fraternity. Louis XVI and his young queen, Marie Antoinette, were arrested. When they tried to escape they were recaptured and beheaded. During the revolution, over 40,000 French men and women were executed by being beheaded. At first, an axe or sword was used, but later a Doctor Guillotin invented an instrument of execution, the guillotine, which is named after him.

The revolution ended the monarchy and weakened the power of the French nobles. Now the French people held the power. The revolution frightened other monarchs and noblemen in Europe, who now feared revolution in their own countries. They were terrified that they might not only lose their thrones and palaces and lands, but even their very lives. But though the revolution struck terror in the monarchs and the nobles, it gave hope to ordinary people.

In Ireland, the French Revolution led to the formation of the United Irishmen in 1791. This organisation's aim was to break the ties between Britain and Ireland. If that were achieved, Ireland could govern itself to the betterment of its entire people, Catholic and Protestant alike.

The most important founder member of the United Irishmen was a Protestant, Theobald Wolfe Tone. He was influenced by the French Revolution and believed that Ireland should be a republic in which all people were equal. Fearful of a revolution, the Irish parliament reluctantly reformed some Penal Laws. But this did not satisfy the United Irishmen. They concluded that there would have to be a revolution in order to achieve their aims.

The authorities reacted by forming Protestant militias to suppress such a revolution. These militias ruthlessly pursued the United Irishmen and their supporters, who were usually identified by their short-cropped hair from which they earned the nickname 'Croppies'. In France, the nobles as well as the king had worn their hair long, and so long hair was seen as a sign of power and privilege. During the French Revolution the revolutionaries cut their hair short to distinguish themselves from the nobles and the monarchy. The United Irishmen also cut their hair short as a sign of their support for the French revolutionaries.

The United Irishmen, as often happened before in Irish history, were betrayed by an informer. Many of the leaders were arrested, including Lord Edward Fitzgerald, a member of the Norman family of Kildare. He was injured during his arrest and later died in prison from his wounds. Wolfe Tone escaped arrest and fled to America from where he made his way to France. He asked for help from the French revolutionaries to support a revolution in Ireland, and the French agreed to help. On 15 December 1796, a fleet of forty-three ships, one of which carried Wolfe Tone, set sail from France with 15,000 men.

Unfortunately, as had happened with the Spanish Armadas, a storm blew up and the ships were scattered. Only sixteen reached Bantry Bay, County Cork, where bad weather prevented them from landing. On 28 December they were forced to return to France. Wolfe Tone was bitterly disappointed but on arriving back in France he sought further help.

Ireland's Darkest Time

In Ireland, the militias continued their brutality against anyone they considered an enemy. The authorities, rather than taking action to stop this, actively encouraged it. This made the United Irishmen more determined than ever to rebel. However, just when rebellion was planned, the leaders in Dublin were arrested. Despite this, the United Irishmen rose in Leinster on 23 May 1798, but were quickly defeated. In Ulster, the rebels, under the leadership of Henry Joy McCracken and Henry Munro, were also defeated. The only rising, which had some success, took place in Wexford.

When his church at Boolavogue, near Enniscorthy, was burned, the priest, Father John Murphy, urged the people to rebel. He told them that it would be better to die fighting than to suffer continual brutality. Thousands of men rallied around him. Some had guns, but most were armed only with farm implements and pikes. These were spears with a hooked blade and were made by local blacksmiths. Despite being so poorly armed, the rebels captured Enniscorthy, Wexford and Gorey. They also captured New Ross, but were forced to retreat from there.

General Lake, who was in charge of the English forces, marched south from Dublin with reinforcements and artillery. The two armies met at Vinegar Hill on 21 June 1798. After fierce, bloody fighting, the Wexfordmen were defeated. Father Murphy and the other leaders were executed, with the priest's body being burned. All the captured towns were retaken and Lake's soldiers wreaked vengeance on the local population, killing innocent men, women and children.

When it seemed as if all hope had gone with the defeat of the Wexford rebels, another French expedition arrived at Killala Bay, County Mayo, in August. It was led by General Humbert, who now marched through Mayo. Locals joined his forces and they marched to Castlebar. The local garrison, on seeing the enemy approach, ran away, an event known as 'The Races of Castlebar'.

Humbert marched east and reached Ballinamuck, County Longford, where he encountered a large English army under Lake and Cornwallis. In the ensuing battle, he was defeated with heavy losses. The French were allowed to return home, but the Irish were not treated so lightly.

Hundreds of the rebels were hanged, and again the English soldiers acted against the Irish population with great brutality.

The end of the 1798 rebellion came a few days afterwards when yet another French expedition arrived in Lough Swilly, off the coast of Derry. Wolfe Tone was on board the *Hoche*, the largest ship in the fleet. After fierce fighting, the fleet was captured and Wolfe Tone was arrested. He was tried and convicted of treason, and sentenced to be hanged. As a French officer, he demanded to be shot like a soldier, but the authorities refused. They intended to hang him like a common criminal.

On the night before his execution, he was found in his cell with injuries to his throat and he died from these injuries on 19 November 1798. No one knows how he obtained his injuries, but it is suspected that he may have inflicted them on himself. With his death, all hope that Ireland might gain her freedom ended.

The 1798 rebellion greatly alarmed the English parliament and king, who still feared revolution in England. They also feared that the French might again attempt to free Ireland, and use the country as a base from which they could attack England. The Prime Minister, William Pitt, realised that he could not hold Ireland by military force alone. He now decided to abolish the Irish parliament in Dublin and unite Ireland and England under a single parliament in London.

This proposal was placed before the Irish parliament but was rejected. One of its strongest opponents was Henry Grattan. The English now bribed many of the Irish members, offering them money and honours. When the proposal was again voted on, it was passed. On 1 January 1801, the Act of Union, uniting Ireland with England became law, and the Irish parliament was abolished. From now on, those elected in Ireland would sit in parliament at Westminster in London. There they would be in the minority and would have little influence. The English parliament could now pass laws to further suppress the Catholic population of Ireland, and try to ensure that there would be no further rebellions.

But the English were soon to be reminded that they could not suppress the Irish people. They could enact whatever severe laws they wished, but the people would not submit. The Irish were still a proud Celtic race that

Ireland's Darkest Time

had endured for nearly 2,500 years. For the last 600 years they had been suppressed, massacred, starved and had their land stolen. Some of the finest Irish men and women had been driven from the country. Yet the Irish had never willingly submitted to the tyrant's yoke, or given up the faith of their fathers, in the words of a famous hymn written at this time, 'in spite of dungeon, fire and sword'. They would not give up now and soon one of the greatest Irishmen of all time, Daniel O'Connell, would begin a peaceful fight for their rights and freedom.

20
Daniel O'Connell

Before Daniel O'Connell began his peaceful campaign on behalf of the Irish people, yet another rebellion was being planned in Dublin. It was led by a young Protestant, Robert Emmet, who came from a wealthy family. He had been left a large sum of money by his father and used this money to buy arms.

Because of his fear of informers, Emmet kept most of the plans for the rising to himself. This meant that the rising was badly organised and was doomed to fail. A further disaster struck on 16 July 1803 when one of Emmet's stores of gunpowder exploded, warning the authorities that a rising was imminent.

Fearful that the government would arrest him, Emmet decided to go ahead with his plan. On the evening of 23 July 1803, he, with around 100 men, marched towards Dublin Castle. He was joined by locals, who saw an opportunity for looting. When the group met a judge named Kilwarden, they murdered him along with a young man who was with him. Emmet realised that there was little hope of a rising succeeding, and he and his followers dispersed.

On 24 August Emmet was arrested. He was tried for treason, convicted and sentenced to be hanged. After being sentenced, he made a famous speech from the dock in which he stated: 'When my country takes its place among the nations of the earth, then, and not till then, let my epitaph be written.' On 20 September 1803 he was executed. He was then just twenty-five years of age.

Rebellion had yet again failed. It seemed that there was no longer any hope for the Catholic population. But while rebellion had failed, peaceful means were now to be more successful in gaining some freedom for the Irish people. The man responsible for this was Daniel O'Connell, one of the most famous Irishmen of all time.

O'Connell was born at Derrynane, near Cahersiveen, County Kerry, in 1775. His people were wealthy landowners. O'Connell was first educated in Ireland, later studied in France and became a lawyer. Though well off, he was acutely aware of the suffering of the Irish people, who regularly endured famine and disease. He realised that if the people were to be helped, the Penal Laws would have to be repealed, along with other changes.

As a young man, O'Connell had witnessed mob violence in Paris during the French Revolution. Afterwards, he abhorred all violence and wished to achieve his aims through peaceful means. With this in mind, in 1823 he and Richard Lalor Shiel formed the Catholic Association. It had two main aims: repeal of the Penal Laws and an improvement in conditions for tenant farmers. They were at the mercy of landlords who charged such exorbitant rents that the farmers could barely afford to feed their families. This led to unrest in the country, with the Whiteboys and other such organisations continuing to attack landlords and their agents. O'Connell believed that if he could improve the conditions for farmers, the violence would cease.

In order to raise money for the association, one penny per week was collected from its supporters. The English government tried every means possible to ban the organisation, but O'Connell was a brilliant lawyer. Each time the organisation was suppressed, he simply set it up again under a different name.

To further their aims, the Catholic Association put forward candidates for election to the English parliament. They were successful, and O'Connell himself was elected in County Clare. This alarmed the government and the Prime Minister, Arthur Wellesley, the Duke of Wellington. He feared that more of O'Connell's candidates might be elected. If this happened, it would lead to more demands, and perhaps even to another rebellion if the demands were not granted.

Wellesley was born in Ireland, but did not regard himself as an Irishman. He once declared that 'being born in a stable did not make a man a horse'. He was responsible for the defeat of Napoleon at Waterloo in 1815, and so popularised the wearing of rubber boots that wellington boots are named after him. He concluded that to prevent rebellion in Ireland, the English parliament would have to grant rights to Irish Catholics. His government drew up a Catholic Relief Bill, which became law in April 1829. This granted Catholic Emancipation and abolished most of the Penal Laws. Only the highest positions in government were denied to Catholics. But the bill had a sting in the tail. The poorer farmers, O'Connell's strongest supporters, were denied the right to vote. Now it became almost impossible for members of the Catholic Association to be elected to parliament, greatly undermining O'Connell's power base.

Gaining Catholic Emancipation was a huge success for O'Connell, and made him the most popular man in Ireland. Emancipation, among other things, led to the setting up of the National School System. However, lessons were taught through English, and pupils were punished for speaking Irish. Each pupil had to wear a tally-stick, a piece of timber hung around their necks by a cord. Each time they spoke Irish, a notch was cut in this stick. At the end of the school day the notches were added up. The unfortunate pupil was then given as many slaps with a cane as there were notches on the stick. This dreadful practice led to a decline in the Irish language, from which it has never fully recovered. But despite this setback, young people now obtained some basic form of education.

Daniel O'Connell, nicknamed 'The Liberator', had gained one victory. But he realised that if the Irish people were to be truly free, the Act of Union would have to be repealed. With the intention of repealing the act, he set up the Repeal Association. Again the government banned the organisation but O'Connell simply re-formed it under a different name.

He held meetings around the country, known as 'monster meetings', because so many people attended. At a meeting on 15 August 1843 on the Hill of Tara, seat of the ancient Irish High Kings, it is claimed that a million people attended. They cheered as O'Connell promised them that soon they would have their freedom.

Daniel O'Connell

O'Connell next planned a monster meeting at Clontarf, scene of the famous battle where Brian Boru defeated the Vikings. It was arranged for Sunday, 8 October 1843, and over one million people were expected to attend. This greatly alarmed the English government. It was becoming increasingly worried by O'Connell's success, and decided to take action. The authorities in Dublin Castle sent armed soldiers to Clontarf and then declared that the meeting was banned. This was a direct challenge to O'Connell. He feared that if the meeting went ahead there would be violence, and almost certainly loss of life. O'Connell, the pacifist who had always avoided violence, called off the meeting.

This signalled the end of his influence. He was now an old man and younger men were coming to the fore. Because of their youth, they were known as Young Irelanders. Like O'Connell, they dreamed of gaining freedom for Ireland. At first they had supported O'Connell, but after Clontarf they lost faith in him.

In 1844 O'Connell was imprisoned, and on his release, his health began to fail. He travelled to Italy to recuperate and died in Genoa on 15 May 1847 at the age of seventy-two. His body was brought back to Ireland, and he was buried in Glasnevin Cemetery in Dublin.

His death was hardly noted by the people for whom he had gained so much. By 1847 Ireland was in the grip of the most horrific event that was ever to befall the Irish nation in its long, violent and bloody history. What did the death of one man matter when hundreds of thousands were dying in mud cabins, in workhouses, along the roadsides and in ditches? Death stalked the land and even 'the curse of Cromwell' had not caused such suffering and devastation. Ireland and her people were enduring 'The Great Hunger', an unimaginable famine that was to change the face of Ireland forever.

21
The Great Hunger

The Great Famine of 1845–1847 was not the first to ravage Ireland. There had been many famines down through the centuries. During the 'Great Frost' of 1740, the country was gripped by bitterly cold weather that lasted for months. The summer was then wet with little sunshine; crops failed and animals died. In the following year, 1741, known as 'The Year of the Slaughter' the weather again was poor, and there was widespread famine. It is estimated that 300,000 people died, though it can never be accurately known for few records were kept back then. But the famine of 1741 was not as devastating as 'The Great Hunger', which lasted for three years. Between 1845 and 1847 there was widespread failure of the potato crop. It was so severe in 1847 that this year is still known as 'Black '47'.

The Famine had its origins in the English policy of plantation, begun 300 years before by Henry VIII, and continued by other monarchs. Under this policy, the land was taken from the Irish people and given to English and Scottish settlers. By the time of the famine nearly 90 per cent of all Irish land was owned by these settlers. The original owners had either been killed or forced to flee to other parts of the country where they eked out a miserable existence. Those who had remained rented land from the new settlers at very high rents. Others worked as servants or labourers for the new owners. As a result, most Irish people now lived on the verge of starvation, existing mainly on potatoes. Any failure of the potato crop would have devastating effects.

The Great Hunger

The man supposedly responsible for bringing the potato to Ireland is Sir Walter Raleigh. He was born in 1552 and became a special favourite of Queen Elizabeth I. It's said that one day, when the queen was alighting from her carriage, a puddle of water lay at her feet. She would have to step into the puddle, an undignified thing for a queen to do, but Raleigh removed his cloak and covered the puddle. The queen was impressed with this act of chivalry, and afterwards favoured her champion, knighting him in 1585.

Though he appeared a chivalrous gentleman, Raleigh was a ruthless, greedy man who wished to be rich and powerful. He was sent to Ireland to help subdue the rebellions that occurred during Elizabeth's reign, and was present at the massacre at Smerwick, on the Dingle Peninsula, where 600 people were slaughtered. As a reward for his endeavours, Elizabeth granted him land in Munster and eventually he owned 40,000 acres, making him the largest landowner in the province.

But his greed knew no bounds. When he heard of the fabulous wealth to be found in South America, he went there, seeking the legendary city of El Dorado, the City of Gold. He did not find it but found other treasures, which he brought back to England. He also brought back two plants, the tobacco plant and the potato plant.

There is an amusing story told about him smoking. One day, while sitting in his garden smoking his pipe, a servant saw the smoke rising. Thinking her master was on fire she threw a bucket of water over him. It's claimed that this happened while he was living in Ireland, but we have no proof of this. What we do know is that after Elizabeth's death he fell out of favour with King James, who had him imprisoned. Eventually, he was beheaded on 29 October 1618, perhaps deservedly so, for he had been responsible for a great many deaths in Ireland and elsewhere.

After the potato plant was brought from South America, it was introduced into Ireland, where a variety known as the Lumper became the staple food of the poor. It grew well in the Irish climate, produced a fine yield from a small area of land, and was nourishing and filling. It could also be safely stored over the winter. For those with very little land, and who couldn't afford to buy food, the potato was the ideal crop.

By 1845 the population of Ireland had risen to around 8 million. The vast majority of these were Irish Catholics, and they were desperately poor. They lived, for the most part, in mud cabins and were almost completely dependant on the potato for food. Even those who were tenant farmers were poor. Most of their land was used to grow grain, which was then sold to raise money to pay the high rents.

One of the Penal Laws forbade a Catholic from leaving his land to his eldest son. Instead, it had to be divided between all of his sons. The eldest son could only inherit the land if he became a Protestant. This policy meant that the amount of land owned by individual Catholics got smaller and smaller. By the time of the Famine, Catholic landowners were almost as poor as the labourers who worked for them, and were also dependant on the potato for food. With millions dependant on the potato, if anything happened to the crop then the Irish poor faced a catastrophe. From previous famines, the people had some idea of what might happen. But no one was prepared for the scale of the disaster of 1845–1847.

When the people awoke on the morning the blight struck they noticed that the atmosphere was heavy and damp. It seemed as if the sky was pressing down on them. But what was worse than this was the terrible stench that hung in the air. It was as if some giant, dead animal was rotting in their midst.

The stench quickly led the people to their potato patches where the stalks and leaves were already limp and falling over. With terrible cries and wails they threw themselves onto their knees and began to root in the earth with their fingers for the potatoes. Instead of finding firm potatoes, their hands came up holding fistful of rotting mush, the stench of which made them want to vomit. Feverishly they ran hither and thither through the potato patches, men, women and children scrabbling in the earth with their bare hands. But few plants had escaped the blight. Most had already been reduced to a stinking pulp.

At first the reaction was disbelief. Most thought they were in the midst of a nightmare, and would soon wake to reality. But this was no nightmare. This was real, and what now faced the people was the prospect of starvation and death. Desperately, they gathered what good potatoes they could find. But the blight had already afflicted most of these and they quickly rotted. The very poor were immediately affected. They possessed only small patches of land where they mostly grew just potatoes. Now with the failure of the crop, they had hardly any food at all.

Neighbours were always good to each other in Ireland and those who still had some food shared what little they had with those less fortunate. But it was a hopeless situation. Millions depended on the potato. The kindliness of neighbours could not feed all those who were soon starving. Within weeks, people were dying of hunger and disease, the weak and the old and the sick succumbing first.

People hoped that the landlords and their agents would help them. Many landlords did help their tenants, and saved many from death. But other landlords and agents were indifferent to the plight of the people. They still demanded that the rents be paid, and refused to give any food to the poor. Any farmer who couldn't afford to pay the rent, or who refused to do so, was evicted with his family. Without a home, these unfortunate people dug out holes in earth banks, burrowing into the ground like animals. Others built crude shelters of earth roofed over with heather or grass. In these terrible conditions many soon died from hunger and disease. They were not even allowed to hunt on the landlords' estates, or catch fish in the rivers. Those caught doing so were severely punished.

As people starved, soup kitchens were set up around the country. Many of these were organised by the Quakers, who are also known as the Society of Friends. They believe in charity and helping their fellow human beings, and many more would have died but for them. Other desperate people found refuge in workhouses, which were places set up to house and feed the poor during the time of Daniel O'Connell.

Before Henry VIII closed them, the monasteries had been a source of food and refuge for the poor. But with their closure, the poor were left to fend for themselves. Anyone unfortunate enough to fall on hard times was likely to die unless they had family or friends to take care of them. Daniel O'Connell had campaigned to remedy this situation and in 1838 the Poor Law came into force. Under this law, refuges for the poor, called workhouses, were set up. Now they became a last hope of salvation for the starving. Families were separated once they entered the workhouse, and the conditions within were harsh. Yet many counted themselves lucky to obtain refuge there.

Those who found no refuge were reduced to scavenging for whatever they could find to eat. People ate nettles and roots of plants and even leaves and grass. Many were found dead by the roadsides, the green juice from chewing grass staining their mouths.

Daniel O'Connell and other Irish members of parliament tried to convey to the British government the plight of the people. But the government was indifferent, and at first did little to help. Many saw the Famine as a final answer to the Irish problem. Centuries of war, massacres, plantation, brutality and cruel laws had not broken the spirit of the Irish people. Now those who wished to see the Irish people utterly broken thought that famine and disease would succeed where everything else had failed.

While the people starved, shiploads of grain, which could have prevented much of the starvation, left Irish ports. The British government could have ensured that this grain remained in the country and was distributed to the poor. But they did nothing, and so the people continued to starve and die.

Those who managed to survive the first year hoped that the potato would not suffer from blight in 1846. But the blight was worse than it had been in 1845. Whole families died in their cabins. Carts piled with corpses were a common site on the roads and in the towns as the dead were taken to be buried in mass graves without coffin or shroud. Some mass graves held hundreds of people, and all hope seemed to have vanished from the land.

Many realised that if they remained in Ireland, they and their families would perish. They became determined to leave the country, and thousands did so, most sailing for America. Others sailed to England, and even as far away as Australia. But travelling by sea had its own dangers, and many of those who left died before they reached their destination.

Even in the midst of the most unimaginable suffering, there are always those who will seek to gain from it. Men who owned ships offered passage to those wishing to emigrate from Ireland to America. Some of these ships were not seaworthy, nor were they suitable for carrying passengers, or crossing the Atlantic, one of the roughest oceans in the world. Ships carrying Irish emigrants fleeing the Famine often sank on the voyage with everyone on board drowned. As a result, these ships became known as 'coffin ships'.

Even on ships that were seaworthy, conditions for passengers were appalling. They had to endure fierce storms, which battered the ships and tossed them about on the waves. When that happened, people were seasick. With so many people crammed into the dark, stinking holds for weeks on end, disease quickly spread, bringing with it terrible suffering and death. Those who died in the holds were thrown overboard like sacks of rubbish, while those who still lived barely had enough to eat or drink.

Even when the unfortunate people reached America, their suffering did not always end. Those who were already living in America were terrified that these poor Irish emigrants, who were emaciated and dressed in rags, would bring disease and other problems. Because of this fear, many emigrants were attacked and murdered. Despite this, the Irish, desperate to escape the hunger and disease, left in their tens of thousands hoping to find a new life in the New World.

By 1846 the famine in Ireland was so serious that the British government was forced to act. It introduced Public Relief Works, which employed men, women and even children building roads and walls and other structures, many of which served no purpose. The workers were paid a small sum of money for their labour with which they could buy food. But the situation continued to deteriorate through 1846 and 1847, and the government began distributing food through Relief Committees, which were set up throughout the country. In some areas Catholics were given food only if they agreed to become Protestants. Those that did so were described as having 'taken the soup', and were called 'soupers'.

Yellow meal, also known as Indian meal, was imported, and used to make porridge. It was an animal foodstuff and not suitable for human consumption. It had little nutritional value, but nevertheless must have seemed like manna from heaven to those who were literally starving to death. Shiploads of food were sent from America, and even the Choctaw people, a Native American tribe, sent assistance to Ireland to help feed the starving. People in Britain also gave money for famine relief and many landlords also continued to help their people.

But it was not enough, and the help came too late. During the Famine, and in the years following it, it's estimated that 1 million Irish people died while another million emigrated. Such was the impact of the disaster, that just fifty years after the Famine the population had been reduced to just over 4 million. What successive conquerors had tried to do – destroy the spirit of the Irish people – seemed to have been achieved by a tiny disease-carrying spore, so small that it's not visible to the naked eye.

But the Irish people proved more resilient than anyone might have thought possible. Though reduced almost to the role of beggars in their own country, and with most of their finest young people gone to America or elsewhere, they still refused to be defeated. Even as famine raged, a group of young men were planning yet another rebellion. During the Famine they had seen the consequences of Ireland not having its own parliament. Now they were determined, like so many before them, to win Ireland her freedom, or die in the cause. These men were the Young Irelanders, who had once supported Daniel O'Connell's peaceful struggle for Irish freedom. Disillusioned by O'Connell's failure and the horrors of the Famine, they decided that only rebellion would gain Ireland her freedom.

22
More Rebellions

The Young Ireland movement had its origins in a newspaper, *The Nation*. It was founded in 1842 by Thomas Davis, Charles Gavan Duffy and John Blake Dillon, young men who looked to Wolfe Tone for inspiration and began to plot rebellion. The most important of them, Thomas Davis, was born in Mallow, County Cork, in 1814. He composed ballads and wrote articles about Irish history and ancient Ireland. These were intended to rouse the Irish people's sense of patriotism. His best known ballad, 'A Nation Once Again', is a rousing song in which Davis recalls when Ireland was a proud nation. His dream was that she would be a proud nation again some day.

He never saw his dream fulfilled because he died at the age of thirty-one in September 1845. By then, famine was ravaging the country, and people were struggling to stay alive. In the midst of starvation and disease, songs of Ireland's heroic past and hopes for a rebellion to restore that past were the last things on people's minds.

However, other young men had a similar dream to Davis' and joined the Young Ireland movement; among them were William Smith O'Brien, Thomas Meagher and John Mitchel. All these witnessed the horrors of the Famine at first hand and saw the indifference of the British government toward the suffering of the Irish people. Like Davis, they became determined to act, and planned a rebellion for 1848.

Like rebellions of the past, it was doomed from the start. It was badly planned, the rebels were poorly armed, and there was poor communication. As had happened before, the government learned of the rebellion from informers. Another problem was that the people were in no position to rebel. They had endured three years of hunger and disease. Hardly a single family had escaped the spectre of death. They were too demoralised, weak and traumatised to fight. Hundreds of thousands of young Irish men and women, who might have been willing and able to fight, had also left the country.

The rebellion, if it could be called that, was a disaster. The only major conflict was at Ballingarry, County Tipperary, and here the rebels were quickly defeated. The leaders were arrested, tried and convicted, and transported to Tasmania, which at that time was named Van Diemen's Land. Though the Young Irelanders failed in their rebellion, they did leave a large collection of literature, which inspired other Irishmen to pursue their goal of an Irish nation. John Mitchel wrote a journal while he was in jail and it's now regarded as one of the finest jail journals of all time.

Those sentenced to imprisonment, or who were transported, were eventually released. Many of them did not return to Ireland, while those who did so quietly lived out their lives. However, some members of the Young Irelanders still believed in rebellion, though they probably thought that it would be many years before there was another one. But they did not have long to wait.

The English government must have also believed that there was little chance of another rebellion. The rising of 1848 had shown them the Irish people had no heart for it. It seemed as if the Famine had achieved what hundreds of years of war, plantation and bloodshed had not been able to achieve – the utter defeat of the Irish nation. But just like the Young Irelanders, the English were mistaken.

Inspired by the writings of the Young Irelanders, a west Cork man, Jeremiah O'Donovan Rossa, founded an organisation in 1856 to discuss political and literary matters. He named it the Phoenix Club after a mythical bird, which is supposed to rise up from its own ashes. At the same time, a young Kilkenny man, James Stephens, who had fought in the 1848 rebellion, founded a secret society. Its aim was to win Ireland her freedom and create an Irish Republic, similar to that envisaged by Wolfe Tone. Stephens met with O'Donovan Rossa while setting up cells of his secret society in Munster. In order to counteract informers, Stephens ensured that the membership of each cell was unknown to members in other cells.

More Rebellions

At the same time, another member of the 1848 rebellion, John O'Mahony, formed a secret society called the Fenian Brotherhood, in New York. He was a Limerick man, and following the 1848 rebellion escaped to Paris with Stephens. O'Mahony and Stephens met and their secret societies then became known as the Irish Republican Brotherhood (IRB). It was one of the most important secret societies ever founded on behalf of Ireland, and was to play a major part in the fight for Irish freedom.

Stephens, O'Donovan Rossa and O'Mahony began to plan rebellion. The latter had a great love of ancient Irish stories and legends and he suggested that they call themselves Fenians, after the Fianna of ancient Ireland. There was great optimism that this rebellion would succeed. In Ireland, tens of thousands joined Stephens's secret society and took the Fenian oath. Among them were about 15,000 Irishmen who were in the English army. These were highly trained soldiers and would be well capable of fighting in any rising. Irishmen also joined the movement in Britain, and were willing to return to Ireland and fight.

In America, a civil war had been fought in the years 1861–1865. Irishmen, who had gone to America during and after the Famine, had fought on both sides in this war. These trained soldiers were also willing to return to Ireland and fight. By 1866, Stephens calculated that he had over 90,000 men who were sworn Fenians.

Unfortunately, Stephens was a hesitant, cautious man, and refused to set a date for the rising. Then disaster struck. Despite Stephens's precautions, his organisation was betrayed by informers. Many of the leaders, including O'Donovan Rossa, were arrested and imprisoned. Fenian soldiers in the English army were also arrested and many were transported to prison in Australia. Stephens was captured, but escaped from prison and made his way to America.

The leaders in Ireland were expecting help from America, but it never came. Frustrated by this, they set the date for a rising on 5 March 1867. But like the rising of 1848, it was badly planned and was another disaster. Apart from fighting in Munster and Leinster, there was little other action in the country.

In America, some Fenians tried to invade Canada, which was a British colony, but that too failed. In England, a police van taking Fenian prisoners to jail in Manchester was attacked by other Fenians. During the attack, in which the prisoners were freed, a policeman was killed. Three Fenians, who did not take part in the rescue and were therefore innocent, were arrested and eventually hanged. They became known as the 'Manchester Martyrs'. Because they were innocent, their deaths aroused strong feelings in the Irish people. As a result, many joined the IRB.

In London, an attempt to blow up the wall surrounding Clerkenwell Prison and free a Fenian prisoner being held there, failed. 12 people were killed in the explosion. A Fenian, Michael Barrett, was tried and convicted of the attack, though there was little evidence to link him with it. He was hanged in May 1868, the last person to be publicly hanged in Britain.

Rebellion had failed yet again to obtain freedom for Ireland. The people still suffered from oppression and poverty. Rents were still high, and those who couldn't pay were evicted, causing great hardship. It seemed as if Ireland would never gain its freedom from England by physical force and so another way would have to be found to help the people.

Other men now began to look at ways in which they might help the Irish people. Most people worked on the land, but few of them actually owned their land. Instead, they rented it. They were at the mercy of unscrupulous landlords and their agents who charged high rents, and who could throw them off their land at any time. If something could be done to obtain rights for the farmers, then their lives, and those of their families, could be greatly improved.

In 1852, Charles Gavan Duffy put forward three suggestions to help the tenant farmers. These became known as 'The Three Fs'. These were Fair Rent, Fixity of Tenure (a farmer could not be evicted without a very good reason) and Freedom of Sale. However, little came of this proposal and the tenant farmers continued to suffer as before. But another man was determined to remedy this situation. He was Michael Davitt, another famous name in the list of great Irishmen.

23
Michael Davitt

Michael Davitt was born at Straide, County Mayo, on 6 March 1846 at the height of the Famine. His father was a small farmer, and when Michael was seven years old the family was evicted from their home because they could not pay the high rent. The young boy witnessed the eviction and never forgot what he saw.

An eviction, which was usually carried out in the morning, was a horrific event to witness. The local sheriff arrived, accompanied by soldiers and men carrying a battering ram. If the family hid in their thatched cottage, or mud cabin, the soldiers broke down the door, entered the cottage and forcibly removed the family. There would be a great deal of screaming and crying as men, women and children were dragged outside. Often there were grandparents living with the family, and they, too, were dragged outside. Even if they were old or infirm or sick, they were shown no mercy. Once everyone was outside, their meagre belongings were then thrown out of the cottage or cabin. In winter it would be bitterly cold, maybe snowing or raining, and the family would have no shelter.

Once the people and their belongings were out of the home, a battering ram was set up. This consisted of a heavy beam of timber or the trunk of a tree, which was hung from a three-legged wooden frame. Once set up, the timber beam or tree trunk could be swung backwards and forwards. It was used to batter down the walls of the home until the roof collapsed, leaving the building in ruins. This meant that the home could no longer be lived in, and that the evicted family could not return.

With their home destroyed, the family was left by the roadside with no place to go. Sometimes neighbours or relatives took them in, but often people were afraid to do so in case they earned the wrath of the landlord. Many families built makeshift shelters under hedges, or burrowed into banks of earth. Others had no choice but to enter the workhouse.

As a seven-year-old, witnessing the eviction of his family had a profound effect on Michael Davitt. Even when the family moved to Lancashire in England, Michael never forgot what he had seen that morning. It instilled in him a desire to do something to prevent such an event ever happening to another family.

At nine years of age, Michael began working in the cotton mills in Lancashire. This was not unusual, for back then children as young as seven worked in factories. Young boys were also used as chimney sweeps, and had to climb up the inside of chimneys to clean off the soot. If a boy was frightened, or was reluctant to climb high up in the chimney, his master would light a fire in the grate and the boy would have to then climb up to avoid the heat and smoke.

Despite having to work for twelve hours a day, Michael Davitt still found time for reading and studying. One day, while operating a spinning jenny, a machine for spinning cotton thread, he caught his right hand in the machine's cogs. His hand was so severely injured that it had to be amputated. But this did not prevent him from continuing to dream of helping the tenant farmers of Ireland.

Michael was an Irish patriot and joined the IRB. It was illegal to belong to such a group and he was arrested in 1870 and sentenced to 15 years in prison. He served his time in Dartmoor, a prison built on the bleak English moors, where in winter it was bitterly cold. He was held in solitary confinement, and suffered terribly under the severe prison regime. Irish prisoners, especially, were singled out for much harsher treatment than other prisoners.

Due to public protests about the treatment of the prisoners, Davitt was released after seven years. He returned to Ireland, and then went to America, where he spoke at meetings of his hope of obtaining rights for tenant farmers. On his return to Ireland he founded an organisation, which he named the Land League. It had two major objectives: to obtain rights for tenant farmers and eventually to ensure that they could own the land.

Michael Davitt

Though Davitt had been a Fenian, he now believed that his objectives could be obtained by peaceful means. He put forward a policy proposing that people should not have anything to do with a landlord or agent who mistreated his tenants. Any landlord or agent who did so should be shunned. He proposed that if a landlord evicted a tenant that no other person should take the farm, thus denying the landlord any rent. No one should speak to that landlord, or serve him in shops, or help him in any way. This strategy eventually became known as boycotting.

The word is derived from the name of a notorious land agent, Captain Charles Boycott, who lived near Ballinrobe, County Mayo. When he tried to evict some of his tenants in September 1880, the local people shunned him. They refused to speak to him, to serve him, or to work for him. Because of this, Protestants from the north of Ireland travelled to Mayo to help gather in his harvest. Large numbers of soldiers and police were needed to protect these workers, and the cost was enormous. Boycott was forced to return to England and his departure showed the people that they could defeat the landlords. All over the country people now began to boycott unjust landlords and their agents.

The British government's response to boycotting was to pass numerous acts, known as Coercion Acts. These gave the police and soldiers extra powers to deal with those who were taking part in boycotts, and those who were organising them. Many people were jailed, including Michael Davitt, but boycotting continued. It caused great unrest in the country, and led to violent clashes between the people and the soldiers and police.

The British government eventually realised that coercion would not work, and they passed several land acts between 1881 and 1903. These granted rights to tenants, and also provided money to tenants to buy their land. This money was given as a loan, which had to be repaid. Some tenants availed of the loan, but others could not afford to, and the boycotting continued. Eventually, the Wyndham Land Act of 1903, which provided £100 million for land purchase, greatly helped to solve the land problem.

When Michael Davitt died on 30 May 1906, he had seen his life's work almost complete. By now a great many Irish people once more owned their own land. But they still did not have their own government and were still subject to the British king. Ireland was still not a nation as it once had been.

While Michael Davitt was struggling to obtain rights for Irish farmers, other men, just as determined as he, were intent on winning freedom for Ireland. The aim of these men was to force the British government to grant Ireland what they described as Home Rule.

The leader of this campaign for Home Rule was Charles Stewart Parnell. In the 1880s he was the most popular man in Ireland since Daniel O'Connell. The people thought he would obtain Home Rule and often referred to him as the High King of Ireland. But just as the people were dreaming that Ireland might become, in the words of Thomas Davis, 'a nation once again', Parnell fell in love with another man's wife. This caused a great scandal and would have serious consequences for Ireland and its people.

24
The Uncrowned King of Ireland

The man described as the 'uncrowned king of Ireland', Charles Stewart Parnell, was born in Avondale, County Wicklow on 18 June 1846. Parnell was a Protestant and his people were wealthy landowners. Like O'Connell, he did not believe in violence and his dream was to peacefully obtain Home Rule. Under Home Rule, Ireland would have its own parliament in Dublin, but would still maintain close ties with England.

Parnell was a member of the Irish Parliamentary Party (IPP) and was elected a Member of Parliament (MP) in 1875. Immediately, he became aware that the Irish MPs had little influence in the English parliament. In order to become influential, Parnell adopted the tactics of another Irish MP, Joseph Biggar. Whenever a bill came up for debate Biggar would speak for hours on it. This meant that the parliament could not do its work. Other Irish MPs also adopted Biggar's tactic and brought parliament to a virtual standstill. The British MPs were angry at this, but there was nothing they could do about it.

In 1879, Parnell was elected leader of the Irish Parliamentary Party. As the aim of the IPP was to obtain Home Rule, it became known as the Home Rule Party. In an election in 1885, eighty-five Irish MPs who supported Home Rule were elected. At this time there were two main British parties in parliament, the Liberal Party and the Conservatives. In the 1885 election both ended up with virtually the same number of MPs. This meant that whichever party obtained the votes of Parnell's eighty-five members could form a government.

William Gladstone was the leader of the Liberal Party, and he was in favour of granting Home Rule. Parnell supported him, and Gladstone became Prime Minister. In 1886 he introduced a Home Rule Bill, but the Conservative Party and Protestant Irish MPs, most of whom were elected in Ulster, opposed it. Because these Protestant MPs wanted the union to continue they became known as Unionists.

Some liberal MPs also opposed Home Rule, as did many other British people. They considered Ireland to be part of the British Empire, which consisted of a great many other countries. The empire made Britain one of the richest and most powerful countries in the world. The British people were frightened that if Ireland was granted Home Rule, other countries within the empire would also seek their freedom. If that happened, it could lead to war, and an end of the empire. Britain then would become weaker and less wealthy, and might be attacked and conquered by her enemies.

Despite the support of Parnell and his MPs, the Home Rule Bill was defeated. Gladstone resigned, and the Conservatives, supported by the Ulster Unionist MPs, came to power. Unionists now spoke out against Home Rule. They described it not as Home Rule but as Rome Rule, meaning that it was the Catholic majority who would rule Ireland. They still remembered the atrocities committed against them in past rebellions, and were frightened of becoming a minority in a Catholic Ireland.

At this time, too, there was bitter rivalry between Protestants and Catholics in Ulster. This bitter rivalry between people, who hold different religious beliefs, is called sectarianism, and in Ulster it led to great unrest. Though the Protestants were more to blame for it than the Catholics, it still made them fearful.

The defeat of the Home Rule Bill was a blow for Parnell and the IPP. But his enemies were not satisfied with having defeated the bill. They knew that Parnell was still powerful, and would try to obtain Home Rule again. So they set out to destroy his reputation. In 1887 *The Times* newspaper in London published a letter linking Parnell with what were then known as the Phoenix Park Murders.

The murders had occurred in the Phoenix Park in Dublin on the evening of 6 May 1882. Two men, Lord Cavendish and Thomas Burke, who were high-ranking government officials in Dublin, were brutally murdered. The murders were carried out by a group calling itself The

The Uncrowned King of Ireland

Invincibles. At the time of the murders it was believed that Parnell and the Land League, of which Parnell was President, supported this group. Parnell did not support them and denied that he had anything to do with them. Despite this, many thought he was lying.

When the letter was published, it seemed to prove that Parnell had supported The Invincibles. Luckily for Parnell, the letter was found to be a forgery. It had been written for money by a man named Richard Piggott. When news of this emerged, it made Parnell even more popular and more powerful. People began to think of him as the 'uncrowned king of Ireland'.

When it seemed as if Parnell might achieve his dream of Home Rule, disaster struck. A Captain William O'Shea filed for divorce from his wife, Catherine, who was also known as Kitty. In the petition, he claimed that Parnell and Kitty were in love, and this was why he was divorcing her. This time the accusation against Parnell was true, and it caused a great scandal. The majority of the members of the IPP and the Irish people turned against Parnell. The party split, thus weakening its influence in the English parliament. It was a terrible blow for Parnell, and he never recovered from it. He died a broken man on 6 October 1891 at the young age of forty-five.

Two years later, in 1893, Gladstone became British Prime Minister once more with the support of the Irish MPs. A year later, in 1894, he introduced a Second Home Rule Bill. It passed through the British parliament, but was defeated in the House of Lords. With its defeat, hope of Home Rule ended for the time being.

It seemed as if Ireland was entering another bleak period. But this was far from the truth. A new sense of what it meant to be Irish was gathering force. In 1884, a group of men, led by Michael Cusack, founded the Gaelic Athletic Association (GAA), to promote Irish games and pastimes. It was a hugely successful organisation, and within a few years thousands were playing hurling and Gaelic football, and tens of thousands were watching the games.

Two other men, a Protestant, Douglas Hyde and a Catholic, Eoin MacNeill founded the Gaelic League in 1893. This organisation's principal aim was to foster the Irish language, which had suffered greatly through emigration and the National School System, which, you remember, punished pupils for speaking Irish. The league also supported Irish music, dancing, poetry and other literary pursuits.

A number of famous Irish writers also emerged at this time. Most, but not all of them, were Protestants, and descended from English and Scottish settlers. They were known as Anglo-Irish, and they wished to revive the ancient Irish stories and legends. They also put forward the idea that the Irish people should be proud of their Gaelic heritage. Ireland was an ancient nation with its own language, culture and traditions. Its people might not be free, but they could still be proud.

These new groups, the Gaelic League and the GAA, did help to make the Irish people proud of their country and their heritage. Meanwhile, the IRB, founded at the time of the Fenians, had quite a different aim. This was to gain freedom for Ireland by force of arms. Its members were waiting only for an opportunity to rebel but right then no such opportunity presented itself. They could only watch and wait and plan.

25
Seeds of Freedom

The possibility of Home Rule alarmed the Protestants in Ireland, especially those in Ulster, who regarded themselves as Unionists and wished to remain part of Britain. At the beginning of the 1900s these Unionists began to organise opposition to Home Rule. At first, this opposition was political, but later the threat of armed resistance to Home Rule emerged.

The defeat of Gladstone's second bill, however, appeared to have ended hope of Home Rule. Now, others emerged in Ireland who had more ambitious aims than Home Rule. One of those was Arthur Griffith, who was born in Dublin on 31 March 1872, and worked as a printer. He was a member of the Gaelic League and the IRB. In 1899 he helped found a newspaper, the *United Irishman*. Like many other patriots, he wanted Ireland to be an independent Gaelic nation, proud of its ancient heritage, language and traditions.

Griffith was disillusioned with the IPP. He believed that all they could hope to achieve, if they achieved anything, was Home Rule. This, Griffith felt, would simply make Ireland a puppet of the British Empire. He decided that what Ireland needed was a new party to represent the people and which would not be a British puppet.

In 1905 he founded a party which was to become one of the most important ever founded in Ireland. He named it Sinn Féin, which translates as 'we ourselves'. Griffith claimed that the Act of Union was illegal, and therefore Irish MPs should not sit in Westminster in London, but in Dublin. Ireland, he said, should become an independent nation and cut its links with Britain. Irish people who were disillusioned with the IPP supported Sinn Féin, and the organisation slowly grew.

Following the death of Parnell, the IPP had split. Later, the two factions reunited under the leadership of John Redmond. But as the Conservatives were now in power in Britain, and were supported by the Ulster Unionists, the IPP had little influence in the British parliament. It wasn't until 1912, when the Liberals were again in power, and dependant on the IPP for support, that another Home Rule Bill was introduced. By now, the House of Lords no longer had the power to veto a bill and it was passed. However, the Ulster Unionists were still determined to resist Home Rule, or keep Ulster an independent state united with Britain.

Under the leadership of a Dublin-born, Protestant lawyer, William Carson, they threatened to fight rather than accept Home Rule. Huge meetings were held across Ulster, and 200,000 people signed a petition pledging their opposition to Home Rule. The Orange Order also gained new prominence, and began to stir up sectarian hatred. In 1913, the Ulster Volunteer Force (UVF) was founded and had 100,000 members. Its aim was to resist Home Rule by any means, including armed resistance. This was no idle threat as guns and ammunition for the UVF were landed at Larne, County Antrim, in April 1914. Though this was illegal, the authorities did nothing to stop it. They didn't see the UVF as a threat to the British Empire, but as an organisation that favoured keeping the Empire intact.

In response to the UVF, Eoin MacNeill founded a volunteer force in Dublin in November 1913. Named the National Volunteers, its aim was to defend Home Rule when it was eventually introduced. About 150,000 joined, but they had very few arms. While they were attempting to land arms at Howth, County Dublin, in July 1914, the authorities tried to prevent them. The Volunteers succeeded in landing the arms, though the British soldiers killed three people and injured others in an attempt to prevent it. This showed the Volunteers, and indeed those who supported freedom for Ireland, that the British favoured Protestant Unionists over Catholic Nationalists.

At this time, conditions for workers and their families in Dublin and other cities were appalling. While those who lived in rural Ireland had benefited from the various land bills, the ordinary people who lived in the cities had not benefited. Most of these lived in little more than hovels, or in buildings called tenements. These were tall, old structures without running water or sanitation, and virtually on the point of falling down. A whole family, husband, wife, children, and sometimes grandparents, lived in one room. As many as twelve or even more might share a room. They were always hungry and disease was rife. Such were the terrible conditions that a great many children died at birth, or shortly afterwards.

A man named James Larkin decided to try and improve conditions for the poor. He was born in Liverpool in 1876 and later came to Ireland to organise workers into trade unions. In 1913, urged on by Larkin, workers in Dublin went on strike for more pay and better working conditions. The employers locked out the strikers, and the police, who supported the employers, regularly attacked them when they held their meetings or protests.

To protect the workers from attack, James Connolly, a Scotsman, founded the Irish Citizen Army. Connolly was born in Edinburgh to Irish immigrant parents in 1868 and, like Larkin, wished to improve the lot of the workers. His Irish Citizen Army clashed frequently with the police, and with men hired as replacement workers by the employers. The striking workers held out for five months but, unable to survive without their meagre wages, were forced to give in and return to work.

As yet, the Home Rule Bill had not been implemented. The British feared that if they did implement it, the UVF would oppose it by force. This would draw the British army into conflict with the UVF. Already, British soldiers stationed at the Curragh, County Kildare, had refused to take action against the Ulster Unionists. They claimed that it would be just the same as if they took action against people in London or Birmingham. This incident, which is known as the Curragh Mutiny, clearly showed that the army could not be relied on to fight the UVF. Although the refusal of the soldiers was an act of treason, no action was taken against the mutineers. Again this showed that the British authorities favoured the Ulster Unionists despite the fact that they were the ones threatening war against the Empire.

However, before the British government could decide what to do about Home Rule, an event in Europe plunged the whole world into a war, now known as the First World War. The event which brought about this war took place on 28 June 1914. On that day the Archduke Ferdinand, the heir to the throne of the Austrian-Hungarian Empire, was assassinated in Sarajevo. The assassin, nineteen-year-old Gavrilo Princip, belonged to an organisation called The Black Hand. This organisation was opposed to the Austrian-Hungarian Empire, which had taken over Bosnia, Croatia and Serbia, and was ill-treating the people who lived there.

As a result of the assassination, the Austrian-Hungarian Empire declared war on Serbia and the allies of both sides were drawn into the conflict. Britain supported Serbia while Germany supported the Austrian-Hungarian Empire. Old hatreds quickly surfaced in Europe and a terrible war broke out.

The British government decided to put the question of Home Rule aside until after the war. John Redmond, the leader of the IPP, and a supporter of the National Volunteers, suggested that they should fight for Britain. Eoin MacNeill and others were opposed to this. They felt that Irishmen should not fight for Britain while Ireland was not free.

This led to a split in the National Volunteers. Those who supported Redmond went off to fight for Britain, while the remainder stayed in Ireland. Many of those who went off to fight did so because they had no work. In the army, they would be paid, and their families in Ireland would also be paid what was known as 'separation money'. This meant that the men's wives and children would not go hungry.

Many of the National Volunteers who stayed in Ireland were angry that Britain had not granted Home Rule. Others didn't want Home Rule, but an Irish Republic, similar to that proposed by Wolfe Tone. They knew that Britain would not willingly agree to this. If they wanted to achieve it, there would have to be a rebellion.

Among those in favour of rebellion were seven men whose names are now revered like that of Wolfe Tone and Robert Emmet. They are Patrick Pearse, Thomas Clarke, Thomas MacDonagh, Joseph Plunkett,

Seeds of Freedom

Seán McDermott, Eamonn Ceannt and James Connolly. While Britain was fighting a war, these men believed that it was an ideal opportunity for rebellion. They also hoped to get help from Germany, Britain's sworn enemy.

In 1915 these men formed a military council, whose aim was to organise a rebellion. They did not inform their leader, Eoin MacNeill, of the council, or of its aims. They were also aware that, with their numbers reduced by those who had gone to fight for Britain, the chances of a rebellion succeeding were poor. But they were willing to make what they described as a 'blood sacrifice' for their country.

They planned the rebellion for Easter 1916, aware that they were almost certainly going to their deaths. What they could not have imagined was that this rebellion, the Easter Rising, would, at last, sow the seeds of Irish freedom.

26
The Easter Rising

You must think by now that the history of Ireland is all about rebellions. And you would be right to some extent, for there were a great many rebellions indeed. But none had such a major impact on the country as the 1916 Easter Rising.

The date set for the rising was Easter Sunday, 23 April 1916. It was kept a closely guarded secret and even Eoin MacNeill, the leader of the Irish Volunteers, did not know of it. The fact that the date was kept secret caused great confusion.

The plan was that the Volunteers, aided by the Irish Citizen Army, would take over strategic positions in Dublin city. These were the Four Courts, Jacob's Biscuit Factory, Boland's Mill, South Dublin Union Workhouse and Liberty Hall. The headquarters would be at the General Post Office (GPO) in Sackville Street, now O'Connell Street.

The Volunteers, who numbered around 15,000, badly needed guns. Roger Casement, the man who had obtained the guns landed at Howth, was in Germany trying to get more. Casement, who was born in Sandycove, near Dublin, in 1864, was a former British diplomat. He had been knighted by Queen Victoria, but despite this was an Irish patriot.

Germany, which was at war with Britain, gave Casement 20,000 rifles and ammunition. These were sent to Ireland in a ship, the *Aud*, while Casement returned in a German submarine. British spies had learned of the shipment and Casement's involvement. Soldiers and police were lying in wait at Banna Strand, County Kerry, where both Casement and the shipment were to land.

On Good Friday morning, Casement landed at Banna, and was immediately arrested. The *Aud* was intercepted by the Royal Navy as it approached the Irish coast. The German crew refused to surrender the vessel and scuttled it. It sank with its cargo of rifles, depriving the Volunteers of badly needed arms. This was a major setback but not the only one.

The need for secrecy created a second problem. Instead of informing the Volunteers that there was to be a Rising, the leaders merely ordered them to meet for manoeuvres on Easter Sunday. This was something that happened regularly so the Volunteers didn't know that they would be taking part in a Rising. A third problem occurred when Eoin MacNeill learned of the Rising. He immediately issued an order forbidding it to take place. This caused great confusion among the volunteers, which wasn't helped by the fact that communications were poor at the time. There were few telephones in Ireland back then and, of course, there was no Internet or mobile phones. So it was impossible to ensure that every volunteer got MacNeill's order and this only added to the confusion.

The British authorities had also learned of the Rising and planned to arrest the leaders. But when Casement was captured and the *Aud* scuttled, they assumed that the Rising would not go ahead. When MacNeill issued his order forbidding it, the British authorities were further reassured, and did not go ahead with the arrests. The rebels, however, were determined to proceed with the Rising. They issued new orders that the manoeuvres planned for Easter Sunday would now take place on Easter Monday.

On that morning, the Volunteers and their leaders gathered at Liberty Hall, which was the headquarters of James Connolly's trade union movement. From here, led by Connolly, Patrick Pearse, Joseph Plunkett and Thomas Clarke, around 1,000 men marched to the GPO. Other groups of volunteers went off to their designated positions. The Irish Citizen's Army marched to Stephen's Green.

When the Volunteers reached the GPO they took over the building. A curious crowd gathered outside and the leaders stood on the steps of the GPO while Pearse read out a document, known as the Proclamation. It declared that Ireland was now a Republic and that they pledged their lives to fight to defend it. At this, the crowd began to jeer and laugh, thinking it all highly amusing. They were unaware that the leaders on the steps were about to lay down their lives for what they believed in.

The Volunteers inside the GPO were preparing to fight. They broke out the glass in the windows and set up firing positions. In the event that they might have to retreat from the building, they broke through the walls at the rear so that they could withdraw into the houses in Moore Street. Provisions of food and water were brought into the building from the nearby Metropole Hotel. On the roof of the GPO, the Tricolour, the flag of the new republic, and a green flag with a harp emblem were raised. Both fluttered in the breeze, a visual declaration that an Irish Republic now existed, at least in the minds of the volunteers. In 1922, the Tricolour of green, white and orange was officially adopted as the Irish flag.

Rather than instilling the crowd with patriotic fervour, the flags flying above the GPO made them laugh all the more. They continued to heckle and taunt the Volunteers. As news of the Rising spread among the citizens of Dublin, their mood turned to anger. Many of these were the poorest of the poor, who lived in tenements in appalling conditions, and had never had a regular income. But all that had changed in 1914 with the outbreak of war. Husbands, fathers and sons from these poor families had joined the British army, and now their families were receiving the 'separation money' from the British government.

These poor people, mostly women, feared that the Rising would endanger the payment of this money. One can't blame them, for if they did not get that money, they and their children would go hungry. Many would certainly starve. Rather than support the Volunteers, these people bitterly opposed them. They saw them, not as patriots, but as blackguards. Many hurried to the GPO to taunt the Volunteers, while others continued to mock and laugh, still enjoying the joke.

But the situation turned deadly serious when a troop of mounted lancers charged down Sackville Street. The Volunteers in the GPO opened fire. Horses and men fell in the street under a hail of bullets. The crowd withdrew in panic, aware that this was no longer something to be taken lightly.

The Easter Rising

Meanwhile, throughout Dublin, other Volunteers seized strategic buildings. Even Dublin Castle, the headquarters of British rule in Ireland, was attacked. But the Volunteers did not press home the attack, thinking that it would be impossible to take the building. In fact, the castle was poorly defended, and could have been taken, which would have been a great boost for the Volunteers.

The British authorities, certain that the Rising had been called off, were taken by surprise. Because it was a bank holiday, many army officers and officials had gone to the races at Fairyhouse. There were insufficient soldiers in Dublin to deal with the rebels, so reinforcements and artillery were sent for. The British planned to encircle the Volunteers and close in on them once the reinforcements and the artillery arrived. This meant that during the first few days there was little fighting in the city. Instead, there was widespread looting as law and order broke down.

On that first Monday night, looters started fires in the houses near the GPO. Crackling flames lit up the night sky. Windows shattered in the extreme heat. Roofs fell in with resounding crashes, sending flames higher still. Mobs rampaged through the streets carrying away looted goods from shops and houses. For those in the GPO, the situation seemed unreal. They had seized the building, declared an Irish Republic and were ready to fight to defend it. But it seemed as if the British army did not wish to fight them, even though they were few in number and poorly armed.

It was not until Thursday that the British were in a position to attack. By then heavily armed reinforcements had arrived. Machine-gun posts were set up and artillery readied for shelling. A gunboat, the *Helga*, sailed up the River Liffey and took up a position from where it could shell the GPO.

With a salvo of artillery shells, the fighting began. The shells smashed into the GPO and the building came under a hail of bullets. The defenders fired back, but they had no heavy guns to knock out the British artillery. Its shells soon set the roof ablaze. Before long the GPO and many of the adjoining buildings were raging infernos.

James Connolly, in a desperate counter-attack, led a group of Volunteers out of the GPO. But they came under heavy machine-gun fire. Connolly was hit and his thighbone shattered. He was dragged back inside GPO, where he lay in terrible agony. By now, the GPO was burning fiercely and already many Volunteers lay dead or wounded. Shells still rained down relentlessly and bullets tore through the open windows. The situation was desperate. The Volunteers had no alternative but to withdraw. Taking their wounded, including Connolly, they retreated through the holes in the rear wall. They crossed Moore Street under heavy fire and took shelter in the houses. But they were hopelessly surrounded and could go no further.

To continue fighting would mean certain death for many more Volunteers and reluctantly, the leaders decided to surrender. Some of the Volunteers wanted to fight on, but were persuaded not to. A truce with the British was arranged and on Saturday afternoon, 29 April, Pearse and the Volunteers surrendered. Around the city, other groups of Volunteers also surrendered. Those at Boland's Mill, under the leadership of Éamon de Valera, were the last to surrender.

All the Volunteers were tired and dispirited. Their uniforms, worn with such pride and hope and promise on Easter Monday morning, were tattered and stained with ash and dust and blood. On Sackville Street, a terrible sight greeted them. Dublin seemed to be ablaze. The buildings, which were already burned out, stood roofless and windowless against the backdrop of the smoke and flames. The street was littered with dead bodies and slick with blood. A famous Volunteer known as The O'Rahilly lay riddled with bullets beside his burnt-out beloved De Dion motorcar. Waiting for the Volunteers was the armed might of the British army.

Hungry, tired and downhearted at the sight of so many dead and the failure of the Rising, the Volunteers were marched up Sackville Street to the Rotunda Hospital. Here, the bedraggled men were herded into a small area and surrounded by armed British soldiers, many of whom had lost colleagues in the fighting. A British officer, Captain Lee-Wilson, strode among the prisoners, striking them. He was a cruel man and not only beat the prisoners, but forced some of them to strip naked. One man who was humiliated in this way was Thomas Clarke. He had an injured arm and had difficulty using it. Enraged by Clarke's inability to undress quickly, Lee-Wilson tore off his uniform. This caused the wound in Clarke's arm to bleed, adding to his misery.

Night was gathering and, though it was the end of April, it was bitterly cold. For an old man like Clarke, who had spent long years in English jails, this was not only a public humiliation, but also a physical ordeal. Many of the prisoners protested at the treatment of Clarke, but were beaten and kicked until they were silent.

That night the prisoners remained tightly packed together outside the Rotunda Hospital. They were not allowed to sit or lie down. Anyone who did so was dragged to his feet and kicked and beaten. It rained, and they grew colder and more miserable as the night wore on.

The next day the prisoners were marched to Richmond Barracks. Policemen, known as G-men, moved among them, picking out the leaders for court martial and certain execution. The remaining prisoners were then marched through the city to a cattle boat, which would take them to prisons in England. On the journey, the citizens of Dublin came out to watch. Some cheered and shouted encouragement, much to the anger of the British soldiers. But others hissed and spat at the prisoners, angered by their actions. Their city had been shelled and burned. Hundreds of citizens had been killed in the fighting. Most of the women still considered their 'separation money' to be more important than freedom for Ireland.

While the Volunteers were shipped off to prison, the leaders were court-martialled. They were found guilty of rebellion and sentenced to death. Over a period of weeks they were executed at Kilmainham Jail by firing squad, and were buried within the prison walls. As each execution was announced, public outrage grew. Now those people who had condemned the rising, and many of those who had earlier spat on the Volunteers, condemned the executions. The public outrage was fanned by stories like that of William Pearse, who was executed because he was the brother of Patrick Pearse; and of Joseph Plunkett, who was shot minutes after marrying his girlfriend, Grace Gifford. Public outrage reached its peak with James Connolly's execution. Though seriously wounded during the Rising, he was condemned to death. Suffering terrible pain from his wound and unable to stand, he was tied to a chair and shot.

Outrage at the executions was not confined to Ireland. Worldwide attention was now focused on the country. In America, and even in Britain, the executions were condemned. Such was the outpouring of opposition, especially in Britain, that the government ordered a halt to further executions. The remaining condemned men, like the rest of the Volunteers, were sentenced to imprisonment instead. One of the leaders who escaped execution was Éamon de Valera. Later, he would play an important part in the history of Ireland. Roger Casement, however, was not so lucky. Tried and convicted of treason, he was hanged in Pentonville Prison in London in August.

With the leaders dead and the Volunteers in prison, the Rising seemed to have been an utter failure. No one could have foreseen then that it would ignite a fire of such patriotism in Ireland that it would eventually lead to the country gaining her freedom six years later. Before that could happen, a great many other fires would burn and a great many more men would die. Most of those fires, and most of those deaths, would come from the actions of one man: Michael Collins.

27
Collins Plans War

Regarded as the greatest Irishman of the twentieth century, Michael Collins was born at Woodfield, near Clonakilty, County Cork, on 16 October 1890. As a boy, he heard his father recount stories of ancient Ireland, and of its heroes of old like Fionn and the Fianna. This gave the young boy a fierce pride in Ireland and its history.

At the national school at Lisavaird, he was influenced by the headmaster, Denis Lyons. Lyons, a fervent nationalist, told Michael stories about Ireland and its history. The Great Famine and the terrible suffering endured by the Irish people was still fresh in the minds of men like Lyons. Hearing these accounts of the Famine made Michael realise that Ireland would never prosper while under British rule.

The local blacksmith, James Santry, also influenced Michael. He regularly visited Santry's forge where he heard more stories of Ireland's past and the injustices suffered by the people. During the Fenian rising, pikes had been made at the forge. O'Donovan Rossa, who had suffered hardship in English prisons and was regarded as a great Irish patriot, was born nearby. In him, Michael had a living hero to admire and he began to dream of one day fighting for Ireland's freedom, just like his hero.

At fifteen, Michael went to work in London where he met Sam

Maguire, after whom the Sam Maguire Cup is named. Maguire, a Protestant from Dunmanway, County Cork, was a member of the IRB, and swore Collins into that organisation. Collins was also sworn into the Irish Volunteers by his boyhood friend, Sean Hurley. During the Easter Rising, Hurley, who raised the Irish flag at the GPO, was killed. His death had a profound effect on Collins, who was to lose many friends and colleagues in the coming years.

In 1916, Collins, now a captain in the Volunteers, returned to Ireland to fight in the Easter Rising. He was appointed as assistant (aide de camp) to Joseph Plunkett, and was on the steps of the GPO when Pearse read the Proclamation. Following the surrender, Collins was sent to prison in England and later transferred to Frongoch internment camp in Wales. It was here that the man who would direct Ireland's War of Independence first began to show evidence of his extraordinary power, authority and leadership qualities. He organised protests against the conditions in the camp and also met men from all parts of the country who were in the IRB. These were the men who would stand by his side during the coming years of bloody struggle.

Collins had witnessed the Easter Rising and saw why it had failed. Many of its leaders were romantics who wanted to be martyrs for Ireland. Collins knew that they had wished to make a blood sacrifice for their country, but wondered if it had been necessary. Later, he realised that their deaths achieved what the leaders had wanted. They had woken the Irish people from their apathy and shown them the injustice of British rule. Their sacrifice had paved the way for a new war. But Collins knew that Ireland would never win her freedom in open rebellion. When the time came to wage war against the might of the British Empire, it would have to be waged in a totally different way.

Not everyone in Frongoch liked Collins. He was usually at the centre of any physical activity, and in wrestling, or sporting contests, used any means to win, even resorting to biting the ears of his opponents. Many of the men thought him arrogant, and this earned him the nickname 'The Big Fellow'. It was to Collins' credit that this nickname later became a term of respect.

Collins Plans War

At Christmas 1916, the internees were released. Collins returned to Dublin and renewed his contacts with members of the IRB and joined its ruling council. With his fellow IRB member and friend Harry Boland and others, Collins began to plot a guerrilla war against the British. The aim was to achieve a 32-county Irish Republic.

The IRB supported Griffith's Sinn Féin party, which also sought an Irish Republic. Griffith, however, wished to achieve this by peaceful means. Sinn Féin put up candidates in elections and began to win seats held by members of the IPP. One of those candidates was Éamon de Valera, who was born in New York on 14 October 1882. His father was Spanish, while his mother was from Bruree, County Limerick. His father died when de Valera was two years old and his mother sent him to live with his Irish grandmother. He grew up with a love of Ireland, became a fervent nationalist and joined the Volunteers. He commanded the garrison at Boland's Mill during the Easer Rising, the last group of Volunteers to surrender.

After his surrender, he was court-martialled and sentenced to death. Because he was an American citizen, and America was Britain's ally in the First World War, this sentence was commuted to life in prison. Under an amnesty for prisoners, he was released in 1917. In the same year he was elected as a Sinn Féin candidate in County Clare, and became president of the party.

De Valera also became the leader of the Volunteers while Michael Collins became Director of Operations. Other IRB men were given prominent positions and soon IRB men held most of the important positions in the Volunteers. With the support of these men, Collins planned his war against the British army in Ireland. Volunteers around the country formed into small groups known as 'flying columns'. These groups would not engage the British army in open battle. Instead they would strike suddenly and without warning, and then slip away until another opportunity to strike presented itself. This type of war, known as guerrilla war, if fought with the support of the local population, could be extremely effective, even against well-armed and highly trained soldiers. However, the 'flying columns' were poorly armed, but Collins obtained arms for them by every means possible. He suggested that once the conflict began, arms could be forcibly taken from police stations.

Collins also realised that guerrillas alone could not win a war. He needed what the British already had and that was information obtained by spies. He recruited his own spies, some of whom worked in Dublin Castle and elsewhere within the British administration in Ireland. Railway workers, hotel staff, barmen, tradesmen, shop workers and workers in general were also recruited to pass on information, carry messages and smuggle arms. Collins also recruited G-men who were sympathetic to the cause of Irish freedom. The plan to fight a guerrilla war against the British was now in place. No shots had yet been fired, but that would soon change.

28
First Shots are Fired

While Michael Collins had been planning his guerrilla war, the British authorities began to arrest members of the IRB and its supporters. Among those arrested was Thomas Ashe, a young, handsome Volunteer. He and his fellow prisoners were treated like common criminals, and went on hunger strike. The prisoners were force fed, and Ashe died as a result. His needless death angered the Irish people and gained support for Sinn Féin. Thousands attended Ashe's funeral and Michael Collins gave a powerful and moving oration at the graveside.

Further anger was aroused when the British tried to introduce conscription in Ireland in 1918. People marched against it and held rallies, creating an atmosphere of heightened tension. The Irish Parliamentary Party (IPP), which had nearly always supported British government policy, withdrew their MPs from parliament in protest. As a result, conscription was not enforced in Ireland.

Collins himself was arrested in 1918, and imprisoned in Sligo Jail. When he was given bail he went on the run. From then on he was a hunted man. But instead of hiding away like a fugitive, he continued to go about openly in Dublin. He dressed in a suit and tie, and looked like a respectable businessman, not a fugitive on the run. At this time, the British did not have a good photograph of him and so the police and soldiers in Dublin didn't know what he looked like. Whenever he was stopped at police checkpoints, he would jokingly inquire if they'd caught that Collins fellow yet.

The British, worried about the support for Sinn Féin, sought to discredit the party. They put out a false rumour that its members were collaborating with Germany, Britain's sworn enemy. The British used this false rumour as an excuse to arrest most of the prominent members, including Éamon de Valera. Collins had been tipped off by his spies about the British plot and was able to avoid arrest, as was Harry Boland.

Collins and Boland were the most important leaders still at large. With no one to oppose them, they set about ensuring that their supporters took prominent positions within the IRB and Sinn Féin. In an election in December 1918, Sinn Féin took 73 of the 105 seats. Michael Collins was elected in Cork. The IPP took only eight seats, and played no further part in Irish politics. In the north, the Unionists were victorious, and became more determined than ever to remain part of Britain. More worrying still was that they had 100,000 armed men willing to fight for their beliefs. Alarmed by this, the British government promised them that when Home Rule was granted they could have their own state in Ulster separate from the rest of Ireland.

Yet the majority of the people of Ireland had voted for Sinn Féin, whose aim was not Home Rule, but complete independence from Britain, and the creation of a 32-county Irish Republic. This was also the desire of most members of the IRB and the Volunteers. But it is unlikely if Collins believed that it was possible to achieve this right then, even if he defeated the British in his planned guerrilla war.

Sinn Féin's policy was that its elected members, now calling themselves *Teachtaí Dála* (TDs), should still not sit in the British parliament in London. As a result, Sinn Féin members refused to take their seats in Westminster. Instead, those who were still free met for the first time in the Mansion House in Dublin on 21 January 1919 and set up their own parliament, Dáil Éireann. Éamon de Valera, still in prison, was elected President of the Dáil, while Michael Collins became its Minister for Home Affairs.

On the same day, Dan Breen, Seán Tracey and other Volunteers ambushed policemen who were guarding a wagon of gelignite at Soloheadbeg Quarry, County Tipperary. Two policemen were killed as the first shots were exchanged in a bloody conflict that was to become known as Ireland's War of Independence.

Many of the recently elected TDs were still in prison and Collins began to plan helping some of them escape. In this he was successful, none more so than in the escape of de Valera from Lincoln Jail in England. Collins himself assisted in the escape, and de Valera made his getaway disguised as a woman. It was a great coup for Collins and the IRB, but they were soon disappointed when de Valera decided to go to America to seek support there and raise much needed funds.

This was a double blow for Collins because de Valera insisted on taking Harry Boland with him. Collins, who had been elected Minister for Finance at a second Dáil meeting in April 1919, was now left alone to raise money for the new government. He had also to direct the guerrilla war while still being on the run and in constant danger of being captured by the British. If he were captured, he knew what his fate was likely to be: he would be beaten and tortured, and almost certainly shot. The British would make the excuse that he was shot 'while trying to escape'.

The greatest danger to himself and to his planned war came from spies and informers. Collins knew that these would have to be eliminated if he was to remain free and the war was to succeed. He needed men who would be willing to kill others in cold blood, and he handpicked a number of IRB men who were to become known as 'the Squad'. They were ruthless killers, and were to strike fear into every spy, G-man and informer in Dublin.

Collins faced strong opposition to this policy from some of his colleagues. One man who intensely disliked Collins and vehemently opposed him was Cathal Brugha. He had fought in the GPO in 1916 and was a fearless soldier. He was elected Minister for Defence in the Dáil, and so had responsibility for military action and the Volunteers. He was opposed to guerrilla warfare, believing, like de Valera, that you should fight your enemy in open battle. Brugha decided that the Volunteers should swear an oath of allegiance to the Dáil, and from then on they became known as the Irish Republican Army (IRA).

The police, soldiers and G-men now became more active against the IRA and Sinn Féin. This worsened an already tense situation in the country. Collins had many narrow escapes from capture and realised that he would have to act against G-men and spies. With misgivings, he ordered the killing of a G-man known as 'The Dog' Smith. He was a brutal man, but was also fearless, and had refused to drop charges against an IRA man.

Members of the Squad waited for Smith as he made his way home one night. They opened fire with revolvers, hitting him a number of times. But he was a strong man, and he drew his own revolver and fired back at his attackers. Keeping them at bay, he managed to reach his own house and get inside. But he was badly injured and later died of his wounds.

This killing, the first by the Squad, alarmed the authorities, who retaliated with more arrests and greater brutality against the people. They also banned Sinn Féin and the Dáil, raided premises and seized documents. Collins now ordered the killing of a second G-man named Hoey. It was he who had picked out Seán MacDermott in Richmond Barracks after the 1916 Rising.

Hoey was shot dead outside Great Brunswick Police Station in broad daylight. This was intended as a very clear warning to the G-men, and many of them took heed of it. But Collins and his allies still lived with the fear of capture every minute of everyday. It meant that he hardly ever slept twice in the same bed, but had to move to a different safe house each day. He was always in danger of betrayal and whenever a spy was uncovered the Squad killed him. They also killed Lee-Wilson, the officer who had humiliated Thomas Clarke outside the Rotunda Hospital in 1916. Alan Bell, who was employed by the authorities to locate the money Collins was collecting as Minister of Finance, was also shot by the Squad.

The British reacted to the killings by setting up their own groups of killers, known as 'murder gangs'. As equally ruthless as the Squad, they helped to heighten the tension and terror that was gripping, not only Dublin, but almost all of Ireland, where violence was becoming a part of life.

At Knocklong, County Limerick, a policeman was killed when Dan Breen and Seán Tracey rescued fellow IRA man Seán Hogan from a police escort. On New Year's Day 1920, the Cork IRA, led by Tomás

First Shots are Fired

MacCurtain and Terence MacSwiney, attacked police barracks. Other IRA groups elsewhere followed suit. The British reacted by imposing martial law.

In an election in January 1920, Sinn Féin won more seats, proving that the people, though suffering greatly from the IRA campaign, supported their actions. In Cork, Tomás MacCurtain was elected Lord Mayor with Terence MacSwiney as his deputy. When a policeman was shot in Cork, masked policemen called at the home of MacCurtain and shot him dead in front of his wife. Inspector Swanzy, the man who shot MacCurtain, was himself later shot by members of the Squad.

The British authorities were becoming more and more alarmed. The army and the police were losing control in Ireland. Something needed to be done to restore law and order in the country and a decision was made in January 1920 to recruit two new forces to be sent to Ireland. These were the Black and Tans, or the Tans, and the Auxiliary Cadets, or the Auxies. Their names became a byword for brutality and murder, and they became two of the most feared and notorious groups ever to set foot on Irish soil. With the IRA and the Squad in opposition to them, Ireland was once again plunged into a period of bloody violence against British oppression.

29
Reign of Terror

The Black and Tans were recruited from among men who had fought in the First World War. When the war ended, they were no longer required as soldiers and found themselves unemployed. With no work available, they signed up to go to Ireland and fight the IRA. Their uniforms were a mixture of army khaki and police black. As a result, they got the nickname Black and Tans, because the colours were similar to those of a pack of hounds of that name. The Tans, as they became known, were sent to fight terror with terror and could use any means they wished to do so.

Immediately, they began to terrorise the population. They would enter a town or village and open fire on houses and people. They burned homes, shops, public houses, hotels, creameries and workplaces, and even shot farm animals. Soon, they became both feared and hated throughout the country. Despite suffering at the hands of the Tans, the local people still supported the IRA. They gave the men in the flying columns food and shelter and hid them, and supplied them with vital information about military movements. Without this support, the guerrilla war could not have been waged.

If the Tans were brutal and violent, the Auxies were worse. They were mostly ex-army officers who had fought in the First World War. They were hardened by their experiences in the trenches, were not afraid of fighting, and were utterly ruthless. They became even more hated and feared than the Tans, though the IRA men did admire their bravery, seeing in these men a reflection of their own courage.

The Auxies wore a blue uniform with a Glengarry cap, a kind of beret with a distinctive cap badge. Like the Tans, they too were a law onto themselves. They sought revenge for any act of violence committed by the IRA, and their vengeance was merciless. Along with the Tans, they were the visible evidence of British policy in Ireland, which was to use terror and violence to defeat the IRA.

A reign of terror now began. When the IRA killed a Tan or Auxie, revenge was swift. Any captured IRA man was tortured and murdered, a fate which befell Tom Hales and Pat Harte in Cork. In Dublin, Seán Tracey was shot dead in a gun battle. Kevin Barry, an eighteen-year-old medical student was arrested for his part in an ambush in which three British soldiers were killed. He was tortured in Mountjoy Prison and then hanged. Despite this reign of terror, when Terence MacSwiney died on hunger strike in Brixton Prison in London, people came out in their thousands to show their respect, and his funeral brought Ireland to a standstill.

The British reaction to all this was to send more spies to Ireland. These men were known as the 'Cairo Gang' because they had previously been spies in Egypt. Michael Collins, aware of the threat they posed, decided to kill them. The date set for the killings was Sunday, 21 November 1920, a very dark day in Irish history.

Known as 'Bloody Sunday', Collins chose this day to take action against the spies because a football match was being played in Croke Park between Dublin and Tipperary. There would be a large crowd in the city for the game. The Squad would be able to blend into the crowd while they went about their murderous task.

Early that Sunday morning the Squad, in small groups of men, entered the houses where the spies lived. Many were still in bed at this early hour. They were shot, sometimes in front of wives who pleaded for mercy. But no mercy was shown and each man was gunned down in cold blood.

The killings drove the Tans and Auxies berserk. They surrounded Croke Park that afternoon and entered the ground in armoured vehicles. Once inside, they opened fire with machine guns and rifles. Fourteen people were killed and many injured. One of those shot dead was Tipperary player Michael Hogan. To honour his memory, the main stand in Croke Park is called the Hogan Stand today.

Afterwards, the British authorities claimed that the Tans and Auxies had opened fire only after the IRA had fired on them. But as no Tan or Auxie was even wounded, it was obvious that the soldiers were not fired on. They had opened fire in revenge for the earlier killings of the Cairo Gang.

That same Sunday, the Tans and Auxies tortured and murdered two IRA men, Dick McKee and Peadar Clancy. A third man, who had no involvement with the IRA, was also tortured and murdered. The British, as usual, claimed that the men were shot trying to escape. The events of 'Bloody Sunday' created an atmosphere of terror in Dublin. Many IRA men went into hiding, while others refused to co-operate any more.

But in Cork and elsewhere, the IRA remained active. A flying column, under the command of Tom Barry, ambushed a convoy of Auxies and Tans at Kilmichael, a lonely, barren spot on the road from Macroom to Dunmanway. On 28 November 1920, just one week after 'Bloody Sunday', the flying column lay in wait for the convoy all day. When it reached the spot around 4 p.m., Tom Barry stood in the middle of the road and stopped the first lorry. He threw a grenade into it and then his men, concealed in the heather along the roadside, opened fire. A second lorry arrived and a fierce gun battle ensued. At one point, the Auxies and Tans indicated that they would surrender. But when an IRA man stood up to accept the surrender, the Auxies and Tans opened fire again, killing him. The gun battle continued and seventeen Auxies and Tans were killed, along with three IRA men.

This ambush, coming so soon after 'Bloody Sunday', alarmed the British authorities. Lloyd George, the Prime Minister, had recently stated that he had 'murder by the throat' in Ireland. It was now obvious that the British, with 30,000 men, had lost control in Ireland. Their attempt to defeat the IRA, kill the members of Collins' Squad and his spies, and demoralise the ordinary people with a campaign of terror, had utterly failed.

There were more IRA ambushes and IRA men were murdered in revenge by the Auxies and the Tans. In December, following another ambush in Cork, the Tans and Auxies began a spree of looting and burning in Cork city. Patrick Street and City Hall were burned. Elsewhere in the country, burning, looting and killing continued.

On 20 February 1921 one of the most brutal acts of revenge carried out by British forces occurred when a group of IRA men were surrounded in a cottage at Clonmult, County Cork. When the IRA men surrendered, seven were murdered in cold blood, and two were later hanged in Cork. Believing that they had been betrayed, the IRA killed six alleged informers in the following weeks.

In March, Tom Barry and 100 IRA men ambushed a convoy of Tans and Auxies at Crossbarry, County Cork. As the Tans and Auxies fled, a large contingent of British soldiers arrived on the scene. In the biggest engagement of the war, Barry and his men were successful and were able to withdraw with just a few casualties. It was another significant victory for the IRA, but still there seemed to be no end to the bloody war in sight.

Éamon de Valera had by now returned from America and was dissatisfied with the tactics employed by Collins. De Valera disliked secret societies like the IRB, and was also opposed to guerrilla warfare. In May, he ordered the IRA in Dublin to openly attack the Custom House. During the offensive, the building was destroyed by fire and valuable documents were lost. It was a blow to the British administration, but won at great cost, because many IRA men were captured in the attack.

Collins was slowly coming to believe that the IRA would not be able to win this war. Many IRA men had been killed or wounded, or were in prison. They were also short of arms and ammunition. The superior forces of the British Empire might yet win out as they had done so often before in the seven and a half centuries that had passed since Strongbow arrived in Ireland in 1170.

Collins decided on one final assault on the Tans, Auxies and spies in Dublin. He was aware that it might be the final action of the war. But before he could order the assault, de Valera received a message from Lloyd George. The British wanted to meet to discuss peace.

Michael Collins could hardly believe it. He and his small band of guerrillas had forced the mighty British Empire to yield. They had effectively won the war. Now only one question still remained. When they came to talk to the British, could they win what so many had fought for, and given their lives for down through the long centuries? Could they, at last, win freedom for Ireland?

30
A Bloody, Divided Country

The British and the Irish agreed a truce which came into force on 11 July 1921. British forces withdrew to their barracks, and the country returned to something like normal. The people celebrated, relieved to have peace after years of violence.

At the end of July, de Valera travelled to London to meet Lloyd George, but did not take Michael Collins with him. This rejection hurt Collins. He had risked his life for three years, while for part of this time de Valera had been safe in America. Collins felt that he had won the war and was being left out of the peace negotiations.

At the meeting with de Valera, Lloyd George stated that Ireland could not become a 32-county Republic. Instead, what could be granted was Dominion status, similar to that enjoyed by Canada. Ireland would remain within the British Empire, and elected TDs would swear an oath of allegiance to the king. The Unionists in Ulster would have their own state.

De Valera returned to Dublin where the Dáil rejected the offer. However, Lloyd George invited an Irish delegation to talks in London. De Valera now insisted that Michael Collins should go while he remained at home. This was an extraordinary decision. De Valera, as President of the Dáil, was the leader of the country. As such, he should have led the Irish delegation. That he didn't do so left him free to later oppose the Treaty that was agreed, which plunged the country into civil war.

Why de Valera did not go is a question that has never been answered. Did he not go because he knew that the British would never agree to what the Irish sought? Did he send Collins so that he could be blamed if talks failed, or if he didn't obtain an Irish Republic? Collins was extremely popular in Ireland so was de Valera jealous of him? Did he believe that if the talks failed, Collins would lose his popular appeal? We shall never know for certain.

Collins refused to go, believing that he would be of more benefit in Ireland. He claimed that he could be used as a threat against the British if the talks looked likely to fail. If that happened, it would mean the IRA returning to war. If Collins went to London, the British would get to know him and obtain photographs of him. If the war restarted, they would quickly capture him.

De Valera was insistent and, reluctantly, Collins agreed to go. Arthur Griffith led the Irish delegation, which included Robert Barton, Éamonn Duggan and George Gavan Duffy. They were given complete freedom to negotiate, with Collins reporting back regularly to the Dáil. Fearing for his safety, Collins brought members of the Squad with him. During the weeks of discussion, the Squad and British spies played a game of cat and mouse on the London streets. There was an atmosphere of fear and tension, and a sense that anything could happen.

The talks began on 11 October 1921. Both sides made compromises, but the British refused to yield on three major issues: the question of Ireland leaving the empire; the oath of allegiance to the king; an independent Ulster state. When Collins reported this to the Dáil, de Valera put forward the proposal of External Association with the Empire as a means of breaking the deadlock. This meant that he knew that Britain would not agree to an Irish Republic.

Eventually, the British agreed that Ireland could be a Free State, consisting of twenty-six counties. They also agreed to change the wording of the oath of allegiance and to set up a commission which would decide on the final boundaries of the new Ulster state. Negotiations reached stalemate and, at the beginning of December, Lloyd George announced that he was going to declare that the talks were over. This would mean a return to a war even more brutal and vicious than before. Collins knew that the IRA would not be able to fight for much longer. The Irish people, too, would not support a return to war. They had had five months of peace, and would not wish to return to war just before Christmas.

A Bloody, Divided Country

On 6 December 1921 the Irish delegation faced a terrible decision: sign the Treaty that had been drawn up, or return to war in Ireland. Collins and Griffith were in favour of signing. The other members of the delegation were opposed. At a meeting in Downing Street, the Prime Minister offered them a choice between the Treaty and war. Facing such a stark choice, the Irish delegation signed. As he put his name to the Treaty, Collins knew that many within the IRA would see him as a traitor. He turned to Lord Birkenhead, one of the British negotiators, and said that he was signing his own death warrant. It was to be a prophetic statement.

The delegation returned to Ireland, heroes to some, traitors to others. Collins thought that de Valera would support the Treaty, but instead he vehemently opposed it. To Collins' dismay, his great friend Harry Boland also opposed it. Ireland, the Dáil and the IRA were bitterly divided.

When a Dáil vote in January 1922 supported the Treaty, de Valera and his supporters walked out. Arthur Griffith was elected President of the Dáil in de Valera's place, and a Provisional Government was set up. Collins became its Chairman, as well as Minister of Finance. On 16 January 1922, Dublin Castle, the most potent symbol of British rule and oppression in Ireland, was handed over to Collins. He was late for the handover and joked that as Ireland had waited nearly 800 years for this moment, a few more minutes hardly mattered.

British army barracks throughout the country were also handed over. Some of these were handed over to IRA men opposed to the Treaty. They now became known as Republicans, while soldiers of the Provisional Government became the Free State army. There were violent clashes between the two factions and tensions ran high. The prospect of civil war loomed. In Ulster, Protestants burned Catholic families out of their homes and committed terrible atrocities against them. Hundreds were killed and thousands fled to the Free State.

The prospect of civil war drew nearer when Rory O'Connor, the leader of the Republicans in Dublin, seized the Four Courts. In speeches, de Valera supported O'Connor. At first, Collins did not act against the rebels. He was still hoping to prevent civil war. He had been responsible for so much bloodshed, and had seen so many of his friends die, that this is quite understandable.

An election was held in June, in which the Free State government won a majority of seats. This showed that the people were in favour of the Treaty, or at least did not wish to return to war. Rory O'Connor now declared that Republicans should target members of the British army still in Ireland. This angered and alarmed the British government. They gave Collins an ultimatum. Either he took action against the rebels or they would. Collins called on the rebels to surrender. They refused, and the Free State army began to shell the Four Courts on the morning of the 28 June 1922. The civil war had begun.

The civil war was a tragedy for Ireland and its people. At the very moment when the country was about to gain her freedom after centuries of oppression, Irishmen, who had fought side by side during the Easter Rising and the War of Independence, were now killing each other. It was a tragedy of the civil war that it set brother against brother, father against son, and created a poisonous atmosphere of hatred and distrust that was to last for generations.

For two days the shelling continued in an attack similar to the British attack on the GPO during the Rising, along with rifle and machine-gun fire. On 30 June the rebels surrendered. Before they did so, they set fire to the Four Courts, destroying valuable records and documents going back hundreds of years. Cathal Brugha, a Republican stalwart, was in the Four Courts with Rory O'Connor. Brugha escaped with other Republicans and took cover in the Hamman Hotel in Sackville Street. Though surrounded by Free State soldiers, Brugha still refused to surrender. He burst from the building firing his revolvers and died in a hail of bullets.

Michael Collins wept when he heard the news. Brugha, who had fought bravely in the Easter Rising, and who had been seriously wounded, had been Collins' most bitter opponent. Yet Michael knew that Brugha had loved Ireland, and had wanted to see her free. Like so many others before him, he had now given his life for his dream. A few weeks later Harry Boland, Collins' former friend and ally, was shot and died of his wounds. Michael again wept when he heard of the death, unaware that soon he would suffer a similar fate.

The Free State army went on the offensive and shortly took control of all the cities and major towns. The guerrilla tactics, which the IRA had adopted against the British forces, no longer worked for the Republicans. They were few in number, had few arms and no longer had the support of most of the people. They were only really successful in the south of the country, and it was in Cork that they had one of their biggest successes, though it was a terrible tragedy for Ireland.

In August 1922, Arthur Griffith died suddenly at the age of fifty. He had devoted his life to Ireland, and was worn out from worry, stress and work. Following Griffith's death, William T. Cosgrave was elected President of the Dáil. A week after Griffith's death, Michael Collins, Commander-in-Chief of the army, travelled to Cork to inspect the Free State Forces there. On 22 August he travelled to west Cork to visit the ruins of his old home, which had been burned to the ground by the Tans the previous April.

On his return journey, he stopped in Bandon to meet Séan Hales, the local Free State commander. A few kilometres away, at a lonely place known as Béal na mBláth, Séan's brother, Tom Hales, along with other Republicans, were lying in ambush to kill Collins. Both brothers had fought side by side during the War of Independence but were now sworn enemies who would kill each other if the opportunity arose.

The convoy reached Béal na mBláth just as dusk was falling on the evening of 22 August 1922. At they reached the ambush site, shots rang out. The convoy braked to a stop and Collins shouted: 'Jump out and we'll fight them.' His soldiers obeyed, and both sides exchanged volleys of gunfire. During the exchange, Collins was hit in the head by a bullet and killed.

His body was brought to Cork and from there by boat to Dublin. He was buried in Glasnevin Cemetery, where his great boyhood hero, O'Dononvan Rossa, had been buried seven years before. His death was a tragedy for Ireland. He had been a great man, and had he lived would have done more great things for Ireland. But alas, his fate was to die from a bullet fired by someone who had fought for him and who, one year before, would have gladly given his life for him.

The civil war did not end with Collins' death. It continued with great brutality, and with many terrible atrocities, until the following May. By then Séan Hales, Rory O'Connor, Liam Lynch (leader of the Munster Republicans), Erskine Childers (who had brought in the guns at Howth), and a great many others who had loved Ireland, and fought so bravely for her freedom were dead, either killed in combat or executed.

The execution of Rory O'Connor again showed how the civil war had destroyed friendships. The order for Rory O'Connor's execution was signed by his great friend Kevin O'Higgins, who was then Minister for Justice. Six months before, Rory O'Connor had been the best man at Higgins' wedding. Some years later, on 10 July 1927, Republicans avenged O'Connor's death when they murdered Higgins in cold blood while he was on his way to Sunday Mass.

When Liam Lynch, the leader of the Munster Republicans was killed, Frank Aiken took his place. But the Republicans had lost heart and Aiken advised them that they should give up their struggle. Demoralised, and aware that they could not win, they did give up and the civil war ended.

31
A New Nation

É amon de Valera and the Republicans had rejected the Treaty and the Free State. When the civil war ended they took no part in the Free State government, which was led by William T. Cosgrave. De Valera was also blamed for Michael Collins' death. While it is unlikely that he had any part in the killing, nevertheless his opposition to the Treaty helped to create the atmosphere in which hatred of Collins intensified. By sending Collins to London, and then rejecting the Treaty, de Valera had indeed helped to sign Collins' death warrant.

In 1926, de Valera and his supporters founded the Fianna Fáil party, also known as the Republican Party. In an election in 1932, Fianna Fáil was elected and de Valera became the leader of the Irish government. This was ironic – de Valera becoming the leader of the Free State that he had previously rejected. It was his rejection, and that of his supporters, which had helped to bring about the civil war, and the deaths of so many of those who had been their friends and colleagues.

De Valera's government abolished the oath of allegiance to the king and also refused to pay money owed to the British government. This money had been loaned by the British under various land acts for the purchase of land from landlords. This action led to what became known as the 'economic war' between Britain and Ireland. Britain placed a heavy tax on Irish imports, especially cattle, which was Ireland's most important export, and this lead to great hardship for the country and its people.

In 1937, de Valera's government drew up a new Irish constitution. Under this constitution, Douglas Hyde, a Protestant who had founded the Gaelic League, was elected the first President of Ireland in 1938. De Valera also negotiated an agreement with Britain in which the Irish ports, still held by the British, were returned to Irish control. In return, Ireland agreed to pay some of the money they still owed the British government.

By now Ireland had reached a state of stability. It had its own police force, the Garda Síochána, a functioning judiciary and civil service, an electricity generating station on the River Shannon and its own radio station. Much of the damage to the infrastructure caused in the War of Independence and the civil war was repaired. Ireland's flag of green white and orange could now fly proudly. Green represented the Catholics, orange the Protestants and white was a symbol of the peace and unity that should exist between them. Unfortunately, such peace and unity did not exist in Northern Ireland where Catholics were discriminated against, and where sectarian hatred of them was encouraged by the Orange Order and Protestant fanatics.

When the Second World War broke out in September 1939, Ireland remained neutral for the six years of conflict. Britain was severely critical of this stance and wished to have the use of Irish ports to protect their ships crossing the Atlantic from America with much needed supplies. De Valera refused to give up the ports, and for a time it seemed as if Britain might try to take them by force.

Northern Ireland, still part of Britain, was regarded as being at war. German planes bombed Belfast and in April and May 1941 over 700 people were killed by bombs. The Irish government, supposedly neutral, sent fire engines to Belfast to fight the fires that raged there following the bombing. The Free State was also bombed by the Germans, most likely by mistake. The worst incident occurred in Dublin on 31 May 1941 when twenty-nine people were killed and ninety injured in a bombing raid, which also damaged or destroyed 300 homes.

The IRA also caused problems for de Valera's government during the Second World War. Though it was now an illegal organisation, its aim still was to obtain the 32-county Irish Republic so many had fought and died for. Seeing the Second World War as an opportunity to try and obtain its objective, the IRA went on the offensive. De Valera's government was forced to imprison without trial a great many IRA men, and nine were executed for various offences.

The war brought great economic hardship to the Irish people. Rationing was introduced and tea, a drink beloved by almost every Irish person, was in short supply. There was a shortage of coal, and turf was harvested on a large scale as a replacement fuel. However, the war did help to heal some of the scars of the civil war, as people were forced to cooperate in order to survive.

The Second World War ended in May 1945. In 1949, Fine Gael, founded in 1933 by the followers of Michael Collins and the pro-treaty supporters, was elected and declared the Free State a republic. Since then, it has been known as the Republic of Ireland, though it still consists of only twenty-six counties.

Despite officially being declared a republic, there was still great poverty in the country, and very little employment for the people. At the end of the Second World War, tens of thousands of young people emigrated each year to Britain and America and elsewhere. It wasn't until the 1960s, when Seán Lemass became Taoiseach that foreign companies set up factories in the country, bringing much needed employment.

In 1967, free secondary education was introduced. Many more young people could now avail of a secondary education and go on to university. More foreign companies, attracted by a young educated workforce, came to Ireland creating even more employment. In 1973, Ireland, joined the European Economic Community (now the EU), which brought great benefit for farmers and industries. It gave Ireland access to European markets and attracted more foreign companies to Ireland, especially American ones, where they could avail of the new markets and favourable tax rates.

The Republic of Ireland was beginning to become the modern country that those who had fought and died for her freedom had envisaged. Its citizens were enjoying the fruits of education and an improving economy, and Irish people were enjoying success across the world.

Our sportsmen and women won gold medals at the Olympics; the Irish soccer team reached the World Cup Finals; U2 was the greatest rock band in the world; Ireland won the Eurovision Song Contest five times in ten years, including a three-in-a-row; the show *Riverdance* thrilled audiences all over the world; Irish filmmakers and actors won prestigious awards; our boxers and athletes became world champions; Seamus Heaney won the Nobel Prize for Literature, the highest honour any writer could achieve, while other writers also won international recognition.

But during all this success, there was yet a darkness hanging over the country. Not all the citizens of the island of Ireland were free. In the six counties that made up Northern Ireland, the Catholic people were suffering from decades of sectarian hatred, abuse and the lack of civil rights. In other parts of the world downtrodden minorities were demanding civil rights. In America, the African American people, led by Martin Luther King, were demanding the ending of segregation and the granting of their civil rights.

These winds of change were blowing across the Atlantic to Ireland. There was a sense of hope in the air. But the winds, as they had so often done in the past, were also blowing dark clouds over the country. In the past, these clouds had meant terrible violence. This time was no exception. Northern Ireland was about to be plunged into decades of such violence that had not been seen in that part of Ireland in hundreds of years. The violence was to spill over into the Republic and to Britain, and even onto the continent. Blood was again about to be shed in Ireland in the cause of freedom. In 1169, the Normans had come to Ireland bringing centuries of conflict and bloodshed. In 1969, 800 years later, bloodshed returned. It seemed as if nothing had changed and that it was the destiny of the Irish people to be always at war.

32
The Troubles

Northern Ireland consists of six of the Ulster counties – Antrim, Armagh, Derry, Down, Fermanagh and Tyrone. These six were chosen for a very good reason; it gave the new state of Northern Ireland, set up in 1921, a Protestant majority. This might not have been a serious problem if the Protestants had treated the Catholic minority fairly. They did not do so. Catholics were treated as second-class citizens, which was a recipe for disaster.

Despite being in the majority, the Protestants could not forget the atrocities of the 1641 rebellion, or the siege of Derry, or other nationalist rebellions. They lived in fear of the Catholics and did everything in their power to ensure that they did not pose a threat. They were also wary of the Free State (later the Republic of Ireland), which laid claim to the six counties of Northern Ireland.

As a result, the Northern Protestants had a 'siege mentality' and felt under constant threat from Catholics, both in the north and the south. This 'siege mentality' led them to devise a system of government in Northern Ireland in which they were guaranteed political power. In the city of Derry, for example, which had a Catholic majority, the Protestants introduced a system whereby they had extra votes. Called gerrymandering, it ensured that the Protestant minority held power.

Having power is not a problem if that power is used fairly. But the Protestants abused their power, using it to consolidate their own wealth and influence, while ensuring that Catholics remained second-class citizens. They were denied jobs, lived in the worst housing, and were discriminated against in education and other areas of life. The Royal Ulster Constabulary (RUC), the police force, which consisted almost wholly of Protestants, also discriminated against Catholics. Another group of supposed upholders of the law was the part-time B-Specials. This force was Protestant and most members hated Catholics. They, along with the sectarian Orange Order, did much to subdue the Catholics and to sow the seeds of bitter resentment in them.

The Protestants celebrated certain historical events each year. Two of the most important events were the lifting of the siege of Derry and the victory of King William at the Battle of the Boyne. To commemorate these successes, the Orange Order paraded through the cities, towns and villages of Northern Ireland, including the Catholic areas. They subjected the Catholics to intimidation and often rampaged through Catholic areas, breaking windows and attacking any Catholic who crossed their path. The B-specials raided Catholic homes, wrecking them in the process. Anyone who resisted was beaten up and arrested.

By the late 1960s this situation had existed for nearly fifty years. Britain, which had set up the Northern Irish state, and which was still responsible for certain aspects of government, ignored the abuse of the Catholics. The Irish government also ignored them, though it's difficult to know what they could have done to help. With no one willing to help them, it is not surprising that the Catholics in Northern Ireland felt abandoned by both governments. Feeling forsaken, their resentment against the Protestants continued to fester.

In the 1950s and 1960s the question of civil rights became an issue around the world. In countries where civil rights were denied, those denied their rights began to demand them. In the 1960s, Catholics in Northern Ireland also began to campaign for civil rights. Among those who campaigned on their behalf were John Hume, Ivan Cooper and Bernadette Devlin.

In 1967, the Northern Ireland Civil Rights Association (NICRA) was founded and organised protest marches against discrimination. This alarmed the Protestants, who were frightened of losing their power. They reacted violently, using the RUC and the B-specials to attack the marchers. The marchers were also attacked by vicious Protestant extremists and members of the Orange Order, whose violence was ignored by the police and the authorities.

As had happened in the 1920s, Catholic families were burned out of their homes by Protestants, who were supported and encouraged by Protestant extremists like Ian Paisley, who preached hatred against Catholics. The RUC and B-Specials did not protect the Catholics. Instead, local Catholics tried to protect their own people and this gave the IRA a motive to become active.

When the civil war ended in 1923, the IRA had not disbanded. Though later banned by de Valera, they continued to exist as an illegal organisation. Military action was rare, though it did occur at times. One such action occurred on New Year's Day, 1957, when a group of IRA men seeking to obtain arms, attacked a police barracks in County Fermanagh. Two of their members, Fergal O'Hanlon and Seán South were killed. Sinn Féin, the political wing of the IRA, still existed, but had little electoral success. They had adopted a non-militant policy and aspired to obtain their aim of a 32-county Irish Republic by political means.

Now the IRA in Northern Ireland began to protect Catholics from Protestant mobs. Some IRA members, along with members of Sinn Féin, disagreed with this, and the two organisations split. The breakaway group formed the Provisional IRA, or the Provos. Sinn Féin also split, with the hard-liners supporting the Provisional IRA.

Rioting broke out in Northern Ireland as violence became a part of life. When the situation threatened to get out of control, the British government was forced to act. They sent the army to Northern Ireland to protect the Catholics, and to try and restore peace. At first the soldiers were welcomed by Catholics, but as the Provisional IRA became more active, the British introduced internment. Hundreds of Catholics were arrested and imprisoned without trial. However, few Protestants suffered this fate.

Some of those Catholics arrested were active in the Provisional IRA, but many were innocent of any involvement in violence. The internees were treated cruelly and many subjected to what amounted to torture. This drove more young Catholics into the Provisional IRA and violence escalated, with bombs now being planted in shops and public houses, and in cars parked on the streets. People from all sections of the community, along with Provisional IRA men, Protestant extremists, RUC men, B-Specials and British soldiers, were killed in the violence.

On Sunday 30 January 1972, one of the most notorious events of what was to become known as 'The Troubles' took place. A civil rights and anti-internment march was organised in Derry. The British Parachute Regiment, elite soldiers in the British army, was on the streets to keep the peace. They opened fire indiscriminately on the marchers, killing thirteen innocent people. Another victim died later.

This Sunday, like that November Sunday in 1921 when the Tans opened fire in Croke Park was also to become known as 'Bloody Sunday'. Again, the soldiers claimed that they had been fired upon by the Provisional IRA, but no evidence of this has ever been produced, and no soldier was even injured.

The killing of innocent, unarmed civilians by crack British troops, which was shown on television, sent shockwaves around the world. It led to even more Catholics joining the Provisional IRA, and drew more support from the Catholic community. The British government was forced to take further action, and in March 1972 they suspended the Northern Ireland parliament and began direct rule from Westminster. They also tried to negotiate a cessation of violence with the Provisional IRA, but the talks failed. An attempt to set up a power-sharing administration, where Catholics and Protestants would govern together, was brought down by a Protestant workers' strike, which brought Northern Ireland to a standstill.

Violence escalated. The Provisional IRA continued the campaign of violence. Protestant organisations like the Ulster Defence Association (UDA) and the Ulster Volunteer Force (UVF) also became more violent. Though claiming that they only targeted Provisional IRA men, most of their victims were innocent Catholics. Their actions led to sectarian murders in which both sides killed innocent civilians in acts of revenge for other killings. Widespread rioting in the cities and towns continued and nearly 500 people died from violence in Northern Ireland in 1972.

The republic escaped the violence until 1974 when, on 17 May, car bombs exploded in Dublin and Monaghan. Thirty-three people were killed in the attacks, the highest number of casualties in any single day of violence during the thirty-odd years of the troubles. Even today it is still not known who was responsible for these two atrocities.

The Provisional IRA also took their campaign of violence to England, where members of the defence forces, members of the government and innocent people were killed. Attacks on British army personnel were also carried out on the continent. The death toll rose without any solution to the terror seeming imminent.

In 1981, Provisional IRA prisoners in Long Kesh prison outside Belfast went on hunger strike. They wanted to be treated not as criminals but as prisoners of war. The British government refused to grant the prisoners' demands and ten hunger strikers died over the summer months. Once more, Britain came under scrutiny around the world, and many governments voiced their concerns about the continuing situation in Northern Ireland.

But public or world opinion did nothing to prevent the violence. Bombings, murders and rioting continued. Terrible atrocities were committed by both sides and sectarian hatred increased. The commemorative marches by Orangemen brought more violence. There seemed to be little hope of an end to the killings and destruction.

Behind the scenes, attempts were made to talk with Gerry Adams and Martin McGuinness, who were now the leaders of Sinn Féin, which supported the campaign by the Provisional IRA. John Hume, who had been involved with the original civil rights' movement, and was now the leader of the Social Democratic and Labour Party (SDLP) in Northern Ireland, was involved in these secret talks. The Irish and British governments were also secretly involved, and these talks led to what became known as the Downing Street Declaration in 1993.

This document stated that the people of Northern Ireland, Protestant and Catholic alike, should decide their own fate. A 32-county Ireland could only come into existence with the agreement of the majority of the people in Northern Ireland. It stated that the people of Ireland alone had the right to settle whatever issues remained between the north and south by mutual consent. Only those who renounced violence could take part in any talks that might take place as a result of the declaration.

The Troubles

The following year the Provisional IRA declared a ceasefire, which meant that Sinn Féin could take part in talks. There was much opposition to talks, especially from sections of the Unionist and Nationalist population, from the Orange Order and from some of the paramilitary groups, which had sprung up on both sides, and which wished to continue their campaigns of violence.

However, with encouragement from the American President, talks began between the main parties in Northern Ireland, with the exception of the Democratic Unionist Party (DUP) led by Ian Paisley. He was opposed to any involvement in talks with the Irish government, or Sinn Féin, or with any party that supported violence. However, the talks were completed on Good Friday, 10 April 1998, and resulted in an agreement known as the Good Friday Agreement.

Its main declarations were: that the people of Northern Ireland alone could decide their future; all parties would agree to pursue their aims by peaceful means; that a Northern Assembly would be set up with parties sharing power depending on the number of votes they received; the Republic of Ireland would give up its claim to Northern Ireland; there would be cooperation between the republic and Northern Ireland with the setting up of various councils; paramilitary organisations would decommission their weapons and paramilitary prisoners would be given early release; there would be a withdrawal of British troops and reform of the RUC.

Talks continued to try and agree on how these proposals would be put into operation. There were major disagreements on decommissioning and policing and the release of prisoners, and also with ongoing paramilitary activity. Eventually, these difficulties were resolved. The Assembly and the Power-Sharing Executive were established in December 1999, but soon encountered problems, especially over the question of decommissioning. This led to the suspension of both bodies. In 2003, new elections were held, and the DUP won the majority of Unionist seats. This party had been opposed to the Assembly and the Power-Sharing Executive, and it now seemed as if both were doomed.

But to everyone's surprise, Ian Paisley agreed to talks between his party and Sinn Féin. This decision of Paisley's had been helped by the fact that the Provisional IRA had decommissioned its weapons, though their description of what had occurred was that the weapons 'had been put beyond use'. Both the DUP and Sinn Féin had been implacable enemies, so the agreement to talk boded well for the future.

The talks were not without difficulty, but eventually agreement was reached, and the Assembly and the Power-Sharing Executive once more became operative in May 2007. Ian Paisley became First Minister for Northern Ireland, in effect the Prime Minister, with Martin McGuinness as his deputy. It was a historic moment as these two sworn enemies sat down together to govern Northern Ireland. After 800 years of war and strife on the island of Ireland, it seemed as if a permanent peace had at long last been achieved, though over 3,000 people had died during the Troubles.

It is a fragile peace, which has been threatened by those who still wish to achieve the 32-county Irish Republic envisaged by Wolfe Tone and those who fought and died during the rebellions which followed that of 1798. The fledgling government in Northern Ireland will undoubtedly face further problems in the future. But with the majority of the people of Ireland, north and south, wishing to have peace and opposed to violence, we can only hope that peace prevails. If it does, then perhaps we may one day see the 32-county Irish Republic so many Irish people fought and died for, and in which all the people, of all beliefs and faiths, will live in peace and harmony with each other.

33
The Celtic Tiger

From the time when those Stone Age people settled at the Céide Fields in County Mayo, Ireland has been a farming country. Before the introduction of money, a person's wealth was measured by the number of cattle they possessed. Later it was measured by the amount of land they possessed, and even yet land can still be a measure of a person's wealth.

Today, farming is still Ireland's most important industry and its produce our more important export. It provides jobs and contributes a large amount of money to the government. This in turn is used to provide schools and hospitals and houses and roads and transport, and the other services we need to live a happy and contented life.

Yet it is only in the past fifty years that Ireland has changed from a country where the vast majority of the population was dependent on farming. Since the 1960s more and more of our people have been employed in factories that make electronic components and goods, and pharmaceuticals.

Most of these factories have been set up by companies from other countries, especially the United States. They've come here because we have a favourable tax system; they have access to European markets because Ireland is part of the EU, and because, since the advent of free education, we have a highly educated workforce.

With these factories providing work, young people no longer had to emigrate. Now they could remain in Ireland and raise their families here. This meant that we needed more schools and hospitals, houses and transport, and so we had to employ more people in those areas. During the last fifteen years, Ireland has had a thriving economy with almost everyone who wanted to work having a job. All these workers and those who employed them paid tax to the government. This meant that the government had more money to spend on improving services.

With more people now living in the country, we needed more houses. So construction companies began to build houses and apartments, providing even more employment. In order to have the money with which to build, these companies borrowed from the banks.

Now that people were working and earning good money, they were able to buy houses and cars and luxury goods. They also wanted to enjoy themselves and went on foreign holidays. Parents wanted to provide the best for their children. They bought them computers and video games and iPods, and many children were given ponies. Quite often the parents couldn't pay for those things right away so they borrowed money from banks and credit unions and used credit cards.

Now people began to measure their wealth not by the number of cattle they owned – you couldn't own cattle if you lived in a city or town – but by the amount of money they earned, the size of their house and car, and the type of luxury holiday they took. Instead of going to the seaside, which was the kind of holiday families took before the 1990s, families now were flying off to Disneyland and to exotic places around the world.

With almost everyone employed and wages increasing, which gave people lots more money to spend, Ireland's economy grew. A journalist described it as the 'Celtic Tiger' and the name stuck. Other countries marvelled at our success – that Ireland, that small, poor country they had once known, was becoming one of the richest in the world.

For about ten years the 'Celtic Tiger' economy was a huge success. Many people became rich. Almost everyone benefited from a better standard of living. But then problems arose. Those who owned factories had to pay higher wages. This made their products much dearer. Many of them closed their factories and moved to countries where wages were lower. This meant that they no longer paid tax to the government.

The people who had worked in the factories lost their jobs. They could no longer buy houses or cars or go on exotic holidays. More importantly, they now no longer paid tax to the government. Instead, the government had to pay them unemployment benefit even though less tax was coming in. This meant that the government had to borrow more money to pay unemployment benefit as well as paying teachers and doctors and nurses and all those other people they employed.

With people no longer able to buy houses, those working in the construction industry also lost their jobs. The construction companies, which had borrowed large sums of money from the banks, could not pay it back. This caused problems for the banks. They now had no money to lend, so companies could not get money to pay wages, or to continue their business. Many had to close and so more and more people became unemployed.

Eventually the government found that it could no longer borrow money to pay for wages and services and the unemployed. At this point it had to appeal to an organisation called the International Monetary Fund (IMF), which provides money to governments which are almost broke. The IMF loaned Ireland the money but insisted that the government cut back on the amount it spends. This has meant that schools have lost teachers, hospitals have lost doctors and nurses and many other services have been cut because the government can no longer pay. When this situation arises, we say that a country is in recession.

At present, Ireland is in recession. But it is not the first time this has occurred. There have been recessions in the past. They brought great hardship for a while, but with good government and the support of the people, the country soon began to prosper again. Right now we believe that Ireland will survive this recession. It will not be easy but down through the centuries the Irish people have proved themselves a tough, resilient race. We have survived occupation and repression, wars and famines and I've no doubt but that we will survive our present difficulties. One day in the future we will become a strong, vibrant economy again, a country which we can all be proud of.

34
Back to the Future

We've come to the end of our history of Ireland. But of course, history does not end. It goes on, and what happens today is tomorrow's history. In 100 years time people will read about us, and then we will be part of Ireland's history. Those people will wonder what we were like, just as we wonder what the people of 100 years ago were like. We might even wonder if they liked history and if they were happy. That is what everyone wants – to be happy.

Ireland has come a long way since those first people settled at Mount Sandal in County Derry 9,000 years ago. Back then a person might have expected to live for about thirty or forty years or so. Now, our expectation is that we will live to be seventy or eighty, or perhaps even longer, as medical advances are made almost everyday. Our technology is advancing, too, at an enormous rate. Perhaps children in 100 years time will travel to school in flying vehicles. Or perhaps there will no longer be schools, and children will learn at home over some such facility as the Internet. Or maybe they will have intelligent computer chips linked to their brains and won't have to learn at all. But that won't be half as much fun as school, though you might not think so right now.

There is a proverb that says: 'May you live in interesting times.' I suppose all people think that the time in which they live is the most interesting. And if you think about it, it is – for them. But if given the choice, wouldn't you prefer to be living now, rather than at the time of the Vikings, or when Cromwell was here or during the Great Famine? It might have been interesting, but not so terribly pleasant with the prospect of having your head chopped off by a Viking sword, even if it was called Leg-Biter; or being massacred by Cromwell's soldiers; or of going hungry during the Famine.

Back to the Future

Just imagine if you lived back then and had toothache. There was no chemist where you could get painkillers, and no dentist to painlessly pull your tooth. Your father, or maybe the local blacksmith if your father was too squeamish, would pull the tooth for you with iron pliers. You would not be given anaesthetic because there was none. So think about that for a moment. Doesn't it make you glad that you live today and not back then?

Medicine, too, in times gone by was very primitive. There was no penicillin to treat infections, and a simple cut or graze could lead to infection, and eventual death. There were no vaccinations either, and common illnesses like measles and whooping cough could kill. When you consider all that alone, then you begin to realise how lucky you are to live in Ireland today.

You are lucky in other ways too. There are no longer any wars or rebellions or famines here. You don't live in a mud cabin without heating or sanitation or hot and cold running water. You have enough to eat. You don't go about barefoot unless you want to, and you don't have to go to work in factories at nine-years of age, nor are children forced up chimneys. You can enjoy holidays in Ireland, or go abroad to enjoy the sunshine and swim in the warm waters.

In Ireland we always complain about the weather. It's always too cold or too wet or too warm. But we are actually lucky to live in this country. We do not get extremes of weather like they do elsewhere. We don't have to worry about hurricanes or tornados, or blizzards or monsoons, nor even heatwaves, though we sometimes wish for those. We don't have to worry about earthquakes or tsunamis either.

So don't you now feel lucky to have been born in Ireland and to live here? Don't you feel proud when our sportsmen and women achieve greatness on the world stage? When our musicians and singers and actors and writers and artists are lauded all over the world? When our people go abroad to poorer countries and, without any recognition or monetary reward, work with the poor and the downtrodden? When the Irish people, relative to our population, give more in charity appeals than almost any other country in the world? And don't you think that when children read the history of our times in 100 years from now, that they will realise what a great generation of Irish people you belonged to?

That's why, as I mentioned at the beginning, history is so important. Those children, who read our history in 100 years from now, will be our descendants. They will be our great grandchildren. Aren't you glad that they will look back and realise what wonderful people their great grandparents were? In another 100 years from then, the great grandchildren of those children will also look back at their great grandparents and then at their great, great, great, great grandparents and wonder about them. Have you figured out who those great, great, great, great grandparents might be? You're absolutely right. It's you! And if you go forward another 100 years . . . I think I'd better stop because all those greats I'd need to use are making me dizzy, and would only make you dizzy too.

But if that makes us dizzy, think of going back 9,000 years. Remember that it would take a page of greats just to go back to our ancestors who first came to Ireland. In another 9,000 years, the children living then would need a whole page of greats to get back to us. To them we would be part of ancient history. But we still wouldn't like them to forget that we existed, or think that we weren't important. Because if we hadn't existed, they would not exist either, just as if those ancestors of ours hadn't existed we wouldn't exist. It's a bit scary when you think of it – that your great, great – imagine that page of greats – grandfather or grandmother could have died 9,000 years ago; or that any of your ancestors could have died in the intervening 9,000 years. If that happened, you wouldn't be here now reading this book.

So history isn't at all boring. It tells us who we are and where we came from. In the future, it will tell later generations about who they are and where they came from. It will tell them about us.

When we look at the map of the world, Ireland seems little more than a green speck when compared to China or India. Around 6 million people live on the island of Ireland. Over 1 billion people live in China, another billion live in India. When we consider the size of India or China, we realise that Ireland should be one of the most insignificant countries in the whole world. The rest of the world should not have ever heard of us.

But the rest of the world has heard of us. People from other countries love to visit Ireland. They love those mountains and lakes and rivers and rolling green fields, which are so much a part of our landscape. But above all they love meeting the Irish people. In the end, it's people who matter. They have always mattered, and always will matter. Who we are today has been fashioned by 9,000 years of history, just as the people who come after us will have been shaped by us. It's how it has been since the beginning of time and how it will always be. We are making the history of the future now. Let us make it as best we can so that those who come after us can say in 9,000 years time: 'We are proud to be descended from those people who lived in Ireland in that long ago time that was the twenty-first century.'

THE END

Also by Vincent McDonnell

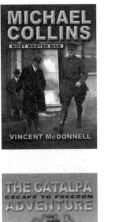